D0814379

MURDER

AT THE INGHAM COUNTY FAIR

By Richard L. Baldwin

Illustrated by Everett J. VanAllsburg (©2009)

This novel is a product of the imagination of the author. None of the events described in this story occurred. No characters in the story are intended to portray by description, personality, or behaviors those associated currently or in the past with any county fair. Though settings, buildings, and businesses exist, liberties may have been taken as to actual locations and descriptions. This story has no purpose other than to entertain the reader.

© 2009 Richard L. Baldwin

Published by Buttonwood Press
P.O. Box 716
Haslett, Michigan 48840
www.buttonwoodpress.com

ISBN: 978-0-9823351-0-9
Printed in the United States of America

I wish to dedicate this to
Past and Present:

Ingham County Board of Commissioners;
Ingham County Employees and Staff;
Ingham County Fair Boards;
and the Thousands of Volunteers
that make the fair work each year.

OTHER BOOKS
BY RICHARD L. BALDWIN

FICTION:

A Lesson Plan for Murder (1998)
ISBN: 0-9660685-0-5. Buttonwood Press.

The Principal Cause of Death (1999)
ISBN: 0-9660685-2-1. Buttonwood Press.

Administration Can Be Murder (2000)
ISBN: 0-9660685-4-8. Buttonwood Press.

Buried Secrets of Bois Blanc: Murder in the Straits of Mackinac (2001)
ISBN: 0-9660685-5-6. Buttonwood Press.

The Marina Murders (2003)
ISBN: 0-9660685-7-2. Buttonwood Press.

A Final Crossing: Murder on the S.S. Badger (2004)
ISBN: 0-9742920-2-8. Buttonwood Press.

Poaching Man and Beast: Murder in the North Woods (2006)
ISBN: 0-9742920-3-6. Buttonwood Press.

The Lighthouse Murders (2007)
ISBN: 978-0-9742920-5-2. Buttonwood Press.

Murder in Thin Air (2008)
ISBN: 978-0-9742920-9-0. Buttonwood Press.

The Searing Mysteries: Three in One (2001)
ISBN: 0-9660685-6-4. Buttonwood Press.

The Moon Beach Mysteries (2003)
ISBN: 0-9660685-9-9. Buttonwood Press.

The Detective Company (2004; written with Sandie Jones.)
ISBN: 0-9742920-0-1. Buttonwood Press.

SPIRITUAL:

Unity and the Children (2000)
ISBN: 0-9660685-3-X. Buttonwood Press.

NON-FICTION:

The Piano Recital (1999)
ISBN: 0-9660685-1-3. Buttonwood Press.

A Story to Tell: Special Education in Michigan's Upper Peninsula 1902-1975 (1994)
ISBN: 932212-77-8. Lake Superior Press.

Warriors and Special Olympics: The Wertz Warrior Story (2006)
ISBN: 0-9742920-4-4. Buttonwood Press, LLC.

ACKNOWLEDGEMENTS

I wish to thank Anne Ordiway, editor; Sarah Thomas, graphic designer and typesetter; Joyce Wagner, proofreader; Everett J. Van Allsburg, illustrator. Thanks to Ken Malkowski, Gerry Polverento, Stan Ordiway, Dave Kirk, Jackie Pelton, Mike Prelesnik, Tom Edman, Michael Gambotto, and Larisa Hutchins. Thanks also goes to Martha Rooker, Marketing Director, and Kevin Brownlow, webmaster.

The idea for this book came from Yolanda Vasquez of Lansing. Yolanda visited my booth at the 2008 Ingham County Fair and said, "You should write a book titled, *Murder at the Fair*. You write Michigan mysteries, every county has a fair, and thousands of people go to the fair." That night, I began this story.

Finally, I thank Patty Baldwin for her support, her listening, her advice, and her love, without which this story and all the others I've written and published could not have been told.

Mr. Van Allsburg is thankful for the support provided by his parents, Scott and Kate Van Allsburg, his Williamston High School art teacher, Mrs. Clark, and his computer teacher, Dana Plaxton. He also wishes to thank Richard Baldwin for the opportunity to work with him in telling this story.

THE INGHAM COUNTY FAIR

Begun in 1855, the Ingham County Fair was held on the grounds of the Ingham County Court House in Mason, Michigan. Admission to the fair was ten cents. Four years later, attendance was over 8,000. And, in 1860 the price of admission jumped to twenty-five cents. In 1868 a constitution was adopted and the fair was now on stable grounds. Over the last 150 years, the fair has evolved into Ingham County's greatest celebration of rural life. Land was purchased, venues were added, exhibits were initiated, and 4-H Clubs were formed. The talents of citizens were displayed ranging from art, sewing, photography, to growing the best tomato or raising the finest heifer. Today, thousands look forward to the annual rite of cotton candy, kiddie rides, games of chance, animal judging, and shows of all kinds. If the founders could attend the fair today, they would be proud and pleased to see the Ingham County Fair in the 21st Century.

one

MONDAY, AUGUST 8TH • MASON, MICHIGAN

A county fair in the heat of a Michigan summer was the last place anyone might expect a murder. A fair should be a place of fun and excitement, the social event of the year for those who live off the land or those who wish they did. The county fair provides a chance to see monster trucks, demolition derbies, and rock bands; to eat elephant ears, popcorn, and cotton candy; and to earn blue ribbons for the largest pumpkin, cucumber, or tomato. But, on this particular morning in mid-Michigan, the piercing sirens and whirling lights of emergency vehicles replaced colorful lights and sounds of a county fair.

Lou Searing, private detective and author of mysteries based on his cases, had marketed his books throughout Michigan, but he had not ventured into the world of festivals, fairs, and art shows. So, he had decided to see if his books would sell at the Ingham County Fair.

The evening of August 8, Lou glanced at his watch: it read 9:50 p.m., one hour and ten minutes remaining to display products in the retailers' South Commercial Building. A customer had just purchased five books; Lou had given the buyer his change and was about to autograph the books when the lights went out. The building echoed with the "ohs" and "ahs" heard in any setting when darkness unexpectedly envelops people.

Vendors took out their cell phones, using lights from the devices to gather personal belongings. Soon Ingham County Sheriff's Deputies and fair personnel moved through the huge south and north commercial buildings, informing vendors and fairgoers that the electrical problem could not be repaired until daylight. Everyone was urged to gather personal items and leave the area as soon as possible. Lou considered the early exit good news, as it had been a long day.

The lights came on around 7 a.m on Tuesday, August 9, as electricians had worked through the night to restore power so that vendors didn't lose refrigerated food. At about 9 a.m. Randy Pollard, wearing an orange and white jumpsuit, entered the South Commercial Building. Randy, a trustee from the Ingham County Jail, was responsible for general cleanup of the commercial buildings in preparation for the vendors' return.

At the west end of the building, he discovered a man down inside the Republican Party booth. Randy reached to feel a pulse on the man's wrist. He found none. He then got in a maintenance cart and drove to the fair office to find Bud Reznick, the maintenance supervisor, to report what he had seen. Bud immediately contacted the sheriff's department which brought the wailing sirens of an ambulance, along with a scene investigation unit from the Michigan State Police. The sheriff also called the district attorney, for he would want to oversee activity at the scene.

Because the sheriff's office had a command center on the fairgrounds, it took less than a minute for deputies to reach the body and to clear the area. Then they cordoned off the exterior of the commercial buildings with yellow tape.

Once the EMS team arrived and determined that the man was dead, law enforcement began efforts to determine criminal intent.

The state police were identifying evidence, taking photographs, and collecting items at the scene that might figure into the potential homicide. Two detectives attempted to locate and interview anyone who had been in the area of the crime the previous evening. Since the death appeared to be either suicide or homicide, the body would, by law, be taken to Lansing's Sparrow Hospital for an autopsy.

Local media crews arrived, prepared short bulletins, and taped longer segments for use during their next half-hour broadcasts. The first medium to get the word out was radio station WJIM. Michael Patrick Shiels interrupted an interview on his "The Big Show" and announced, "There has been an apparent murder at the Ingham County Fair. The Ingham County Sheriff's office reported that a body was discovered early this morning at the Fairgrounds on M-36, east of Mason. The commercial buildings have been cordoned off, the body removed, and Fair officials have been given permission to open as scheduled at 11 a.m. Details of the death are not available at this time, nor has the victim's name been released. We'll give you more information as it becomes available."

Vendors were informed that the South Commercial Building was now a crime scene. They were told they would be allowed to collect their booth materials and wares on Wednesday. When Lou arrived at 10 a.m, he was told by the exhibits coordinator that a prominent judge and candidate for the Michigan Legislature had been murdered. Shortly thereafter he was approached by Tom Edman, the Executive Director of the fair.

"We need your help, Lou. We've got a murder, and it needs to be solved quickly. This will become a bad image on our operations — people will talk about it for years. The sooner this is resolved, the sooner we can repair our image. Would you please get right on it? "

Lou was taken aback. "Well, first of all, I can't get right on it without an invitation from the sheriff, and I'm sure his deputies have the resources needed to work this. They don't need a small-town private detective giving them a hand," Lou replied. "Besides, I have enough distractions in my life without law enforcement telling me to mind my own business."

"I'll pave the way," Tom said. "They need all the help they can get, whether they realize it or not. Like any law enforcement office, the sheriff and his staff have many investigations underway. Having an excellent crime-solver on the scene should be reason enough for them to welcome you."

"I'll help, but only if the sheriff agrees," Lou replied, repeating his condition for involvement.

"Give me your cell phone number, and I'll let you know when I get the go-ahead," Tom said, producing paper and a pen from his pocket. "And we'll refund a portion of your booth fee because you'll be solving a crime instead of selling your novels."

Within five minutes of Tom's departure, Lou's cell phone rang.

"Lou, this is Ingham County Sheriff Gene Lloyd. I just talked to Tom Edman. Please join us. Your reputation is good in the law enforcement community."

"I'm surprised you've even heard of me," Lou replied.

"Every sheriff and chief of police who heard you at our last state conference holds you and your team in high regard. You won the respect of law enforcement officers all over Michigan when you gave your talk."

"Hmm. As I recall, I was afraid my talk might be rather boring to sheriffs."

"On the contrary. We were amazed at the research you do, the thinking process you use to solve a murder, and how you, Maggie, Jack, and Heather work as a team. You were at your best, Lou."

"Well, thanks. Where shall I go to meet someone?"

"One of us will come to you in an electric cart. I'll want to tell you what we know so we're on the same page."

"OK. I'll be waiting. By the way, I'm standing inside the main arena, eye to eye with a bull that doesn't look real pleased to be penned up. I'll go outside and flag down the cart."

The EMS vehicle pulled into the third bay behind Lansing's Sparrow Hospital. The body was weighed and measured for length before being zipped into a body bag and placed in a cooler to await an autopsy which had been scheduled for the next day.

Prior to autopsy, the doctor on duty would review the scene investigator's report and outline directions for those preparing the body for his inspection. Blood would be drawn to test body fluids for any substances that may have contributed to the death. The bullet or bullets would be removed, along with any organs that had been damaged in the path of the bullet. The body, identified by a white tag around the left big toe, was placed inside a grey body bag and refrigerated till morning. The victim had been identified on the scene, so no one would need to come to the hospital to view and confirm who was murdered. In the matter of a day, the autopsy office would hopefully be prepared to inform the police of the cause and manner of death.

Over the last ten years, Lou Searing, private detective, had solved a series of murders in his home state of Michigan. In the first six cases, he had benefitted from the help of Maggie McMillan, of Battle Creek. Maggie uses an ultra-light sports wheelchair.

She drives her own car and is able to transfer from chair to car quite easily.

A few years ago, when Maggie and her husband Tom adopted LuLing, a baby from Korea, Maggie decided that she didn't want to put herself in harm's way. Lou worked the next case on his own, while Maggie helped behind the scenes.

In Lou's last two investigations, Jack Kelly, of Muskegon, has joined him. Jack, aged 62, started out as a fan of Lou's mysteries; through a fluke of circumstances, shortly after meeting his favorite detective in person, he became an on-site replacement for Maggie. Jack serves as a research specialist, and he's a genius at logically thinking through a variety of scenarios in problem-solving.

Rounding out the team is Heather Moore, a freshman at Western Michigan University in Kalamazoo, also a chair user, who a year ago asked Lou if she could work with Maggie on a case. While in junior high school, Heather dove into a neighbor's swimming pool and did considerable damage to her spinal column leading to her need for a wheelchair. After extensive physical therapy, Heather was able to gain movement and strength in her arms, allowing her to use a computer, drive an accessible van, and move her motorized chair with great agility.

Lou himself is 67 years young. He is six feet tall, has male-pattern baldness, and is a bit pudgy, a far cry from his days of road races when he used to win medals in 5K and 10K races. At the peak of his passion for racing, he completed a marathon and took part in a couple of triathlons. Since then, chocolate, ice cream, and all things delicious have altered his frame. He is also quite hard-of-hearing, and wears two hearing aids to enhance communication.

Lou and his wife Carol live in a beautiful home they built on the shore of Lake Michigan south of Grand Haven. The garage shelters Lou's Harley-Davidson which he used to ride often, even taking a trip to the East Coast with a friend. Now, except for a few local rides, the bike has remained stationary. Lou's reaction time is not what it once was, and he had a close call with a vehicle turning left from a right lane a year ago. The scare convinced him that his travels had best be in something covered and equipped to absorb the shock of an accident.

Samm, a beautiful golden retriever, shares the Searing home. Samm once enjoyed evening walks with Lou and Carol on the shore of Lake Michigan, but she took a bullet in her leg a few years back as she tried to alert Lou to an assassin's presence. Samm lost her right front leg. She was fitted with a prosthesis and can now walk with a limp, but prefers a ride in her red Radio Flyer when Lou and Carol take their walks. True mistress of the house is a part-Siamese cat, Millie, who usually keeps to herself, except when she wants foot rubs or occupies Carol's lap in the evening.

Lou and Carol enjoyed satisfying careers in special education. Lou was a teacher, college professor, and government administrator. Carol was a teacher of hearing-impaired children and near the end of her career was a pre-primary home teacher, a job she tells people was the highlight of her career. Now, in retirement, Lou investigates crimes when requested to do so by the law enforcement agency in charge. Following a completed investigation, Lou writes a mystery novel about the case.

Carol, age 70, but not looking a day over 55, is a delightful woman who constantly helps others — in her church, her neighborhood, or through her favorite charities. She is five-foot-two with graying hair and a sparkling personality. She enjoys her eight grandchildren, volunteering, and serving as a member of the Board of Directors for the local Ronald McDonald House. Occasionally, when she can pull Lou away from his obsession with solving crimes, they travel around the world — usually on a cruise ship, on either European rivers or the open seas.

As Lou was being briefed by Sheriff Lloyd, Carol was talking with a travel agent about river cruises through France. Most likely she would not appreciate Lou's jumping into another case. But she knows the detecting brings him satisfaction; so she'll pray for his safety, try not to nag, and wait until he's reached a reasonable conclusion to a case.

two

TUESDAY, AUGUST 9TH • MASON, MICHIGAN

The name of the victim, Winston Breckinridge, was released to the media. Winston was an Ingham County Judge, and also an Ingham County Republican candidate for State Representative. Ingham County is allotted three of the 110 seats in the Michigan House of Representatives. The majority of the House seats were currently filled by Democrats; Winston was slated to be a high-profile candidate who could easily win the seat for the Republicans. His reputation was that of a no-nonsense judge who threw the book at anyone who took the law into his or her own hands. He was much appreciated by local conservatives who believed the country had gone to the dogs and was overrun by people with little respect for the law and those pledged to uphold it.

Sheriff Lloyd arrived in an electric cart, shook Lou's hand, and the two men proceeded to the Command Center, a thirty-foot mobile unit located at the edge of the fairgrounds. Inside, six officers were going over materials, photos, and information provided by people who were near or in the area of the South Commercial Building when the blackout occurred. In one corner of the room, Randy Pollard was being questioned by a detective.

"It appears the cause of death was a bullet wound to the chest," Sheriff Lloyd began. "The judge's shirt was soaked with blood. The medical examiner confirmed that death occurred several hours ago. The judge was shot by someone who obviously used a silenced firearm because no one re-ported a gunshot prior to, during, or shortly after the blackout.

"I don't imagine there were any wit-nesses?" Lou asked.

"None of the people at the fair or in the commercial building has come forward. When the lights went out, vendors and visitors were told to va-cate the building, and they did just that.

"The fair electrician found the lock cut on the breaker box, and inside he found the remains of an emergency flare. He thinks the intense heat from the flare melted the wires, causing a short, which inter-rupted electricity to the commercial buildings."

"It seems obvious the whole thing was well planned," Lou said, deep in thought. "You cause the breaker box to short, as-suring darkness. You have an unlit area in which to commit the crime, and you have pandemonium around the scene. The sheriff's deputies are concerned with safety and crowd control, so they're distracted. In the darkness, people won't see the body. At first blush, it seems premeditated, as opposed to an emotional spur-of-the-moment act."

"Makes sense to me, Lou."

"Were people stranded on rides when the power went off?" Lou asked.

"No, the breaker box fed only the two commercial buildings."

"That's good."

"Yeah, bad enough to have a murder at the fair without adding people suspended in space."

"And, I assume that your officers searched the area and found nothing of interest," Lou stated.

"Yes, that's correct. We have a list of everything found in and around the booth. Most items are campaign-related, but we found things that may have been left by fairgoers: you know, personal items like pens, that kind of thing."

"Okay, I'd like a copy of that list," Lou said. "And, I suppose you've taken photos at the crime scene."

"Yes, definitely. The State Police Crime Scene Unit has all of that."

"Was the judge married?" Lou asked.

"Yes. And, that brings up an interesting point," the sheriff replied. "His wife Bonnie showed practically no emotion when informed of his death."

"Everyone reacts to such news differently," Lou noted.

"I know. I've had a lot of experience sharing bad news, but this woman took it as if I were bringing a piece of mail that had been mis-delivered."

"Well, we'll note the reaction and see if it fits any pattern from the other things we learn," Lou replied. "Let me get this straight, Sheriff: the man was shot around ten last evening; and his body was discovered around nine this morning. Am I right?"

"We think it was closer to 9:50, because that's when the lights went out. But we can't be certain as to the actual time."

"Did Mrs. Breckinridge call you or the fair office saying her husband was missing?" Lou inquired.

"No. I asked her about that," Sheriff Lloyd replied. "She said she went to bed early and didn't realize that he had not come home till she awoke in the morning. But, she also said it was common for Judge Win, as he was known to friends, to sleep in his office. Or he would come home late, catch a few hours' sleep and leave in the early morning. Often she did not even know that he came home. So, she didn't consider *not* seeing him reason to suspect anything out of the ordinary."

"I see. Could she have gone to the fair, killed him, and returned home?"

"Anything is possible, Lou," Sheriff Lloyd said. "I'm confident that didn't happen, but it could have."

"You've got some natural suspects…" Lou began.

"Democrats?" the sheriff grinned.

"I suppose so. At this point in the investigation, we're simply throwing out possibilities. But, yes, his opponent in the November election would be a suspect. Was he or she at the fair?" Lou asked.

"I don't know yet. And, for your information, the opponent is a *he*, Lester Grant."

"You also said some county jail prisoners were on the grounds?" Lou asked, wanting to confirm what he had been told earlier.

"Yes, the fair arranges with my office to have trustees work the fair. Both agencies win; the fair gets cheap labor, and those in jail get time outside a cell."

"Okay, anything else I need to know?" Lou asked.

"That's it, Lou. We're at your disposal."

"You'll alert your staff that I'm helping, correct?"

"They all know."

"Good. I don't like working in other people's sandboxes unless I'm invited."

"We're thankful you're in the sandbox, Lou."

"You know that Jack Kelly will be working with me? And I may need Maggie McMillan and Heather Moore. The four of us have formed a unique team, or maybe 'squad' is a better word."

"That's understood, Lou."

"Okay, it looks like I have work to do, Sheriff. We're going to solve this — the only question is how long it takes. The judge must have had an enemy who sought his or her own version of justice."

"Let me know if there's anything my staff can do, Lou. We may have it wrapped up before you and your team, but we can't have enough minds on a case like this."

The next day, August 10, promised to be a scorcher. Lou put out a call to his team, Maggie, Jack, and Heather, asking them to come to Mason to investigate the murder of Winston Breckinridge. Jack drove east to Lansing along I-96 and down U.S. I27 to Mason, while Maggie and Heather drove separately, going east on I-94 then north on 127.

Jack, with a full head of hair, and a trimmed moustache, was usually dressed in fashionable attire. Age-wise, Maggie and Heather could pass for mother and daughter. They became friends when Heather, as a senior at Battle Creek Central High School, befriended Maggie, looking for a successful adult role model. Both were slim, and like Jack, super intelligent.

The four sat around a corner table at the Bestsellers Book Store in Mason. Jack, Maggie, and Heather ordered French vanilla lattes; Lou deemed that too sweet, so he ordered his usual cup of black coffee. After some informal conversation, Lou began.

"I've talked with the Ingham County Sheriff, Gene Lloyd, and I have our marching orders. I've written notes of our conversation as I remember it. He explained how the judge was murdered — gunshot wound in the chest — how the breaker box was damaged to cause the blackout. He said other things, too, which you can read in my notes."

Lou passed the papers to Jack, who reviewed them, and passed them on to Maggie.

"What do you need me to do?" Jack asked.

"I'm assigning you Judge Breckinridge. I want you to get to know this man almost as well as he knew himself."

"And me?" Maggie asked.

"Stick with me, listen carefully to what you hear, and formulate scenarios that could be involved with this crime.

"And me?" Heather asked.

"I want you to create a computerized case file and add what we learn about suspects to the mix."

After the lattes were delivered, Jack offered a new option. "I've received an e-mail from a woman named Lisa Myers, a 4-H leader in Rives Junction, a bit north of Jackson. She found my e-mail address on your web site, Lou. I don't know why she wrote to me instead of you, but, she's read your books, and she knows you often invite a group of students to help us. Her 4-H members would enjoy working on this case, assuming there's something they can do."

"Thanks, Jack. Give me her phone number, and I'll call her back."

Lou informed the others he would be staying at the Comfort Inn in Okemos, about six miles north of Mason. He told the others that if they needed housing in the Lansing area, they should make reservations, and he would reimburse them for those and other expenses. In the meantime, since the four of them were in Ingham County, Lou suggested they become familiar with people and places relevant to the death of Winston Breckinridge.

Lou and Maggie talked with Ben Morlock, an up-and-coming politician currently serving as campaign manager for a prominent mid-Michigan Republican candidate for the U.S. House of Representatives. Ben agreed to meet at the county Republican headquarters.

"First of all, I'm sorry for your loss," Lou said somberly.

"Thank you," Ben replied. "We're all devastated by the murder."

"Tell me about assignments to your booth at the fair," Lou said.

"It was all volunteer help," Ben began. "I asked our members to donate time at the booth during the week. A sign-up sheet was put on our web site, and party members signed up in two-hour blocks. Judge Win signed up a good ten days ago for the 9 p.m. to 11 p.m. shift on August 8."

"So, it was common knowledge, at least among those with access to the web site, that the judge would be at the booth during that time. Correct?" Lou asked.

"Yes. And the web site isn't only for Republican Party members. Anyone could find out who would be at the booth," Ben continued.

"I see. Was anyone else at the booth when the electrical problem occurred?"

"Karen Scott and the judge were the only ones signed up for that time. I've talked to Karen, and she was not in the booth when the lights went out. She told me she was paged, asking her to go to the fair office for an important call. When she got there, no one was on the phone."

"My guess is the murderer was being careful prior to the shooting," Lou explained. "He or she wanted the judge alone at the booth when the circuit breaker blew."

"How would the murderer know the power would go out?" Ben asked.

"He or she would cause the outage," Lou replied.

"That makes sense. Any more questions?" Ben asked.

Maggie spoke up. "I have one. The most obvious is, Do you have any thoughts about who could have done this? Did the judge have any enemies that you knew of?"

"It could have been anyone, Mrs. McMillan. Judge Win was a person you either loved or despised. A lot of people had no use for him, and some worshipped the ground he walked on. But I don't see anyone obvious."

"How about his opponent?" Lou asked.

"Les Grant?" Ben replied.

"Yes. Could he be a suspect?" Lou asked.

"Not a chance," Ben replied quickly. "Les is a highly-respected attorney. He understands politics, and he doesn't take the mud-slinging personally because he knows it's all part of the game. In fact, I would wager the judge held stronger feelings about Lester than Lester did for the judge. If *Les* had been murdered, I might have accused the judge, but not the other way around. I, for one, will be thrown for a loop if he's involved."

"Thanks. We may need to talk to you again," Lou said, handing Ben a business card. "If you learn anything that might be of interest to me, please call."

Heather Moore checked into the Hampton Inn in Okemos and immediately began to write a computer program into which she could enter suspect information as it came to her. She had found a way to take significant clues and match them to the suspects. She explained it to Lou this way. "Let's say a suspect was seen by more than one person, at 8 p.m. the night of the murder, in a town three hours from the scene of the crime. My program will flag that unique situation for us."

"Computers may someday replace our crime-fighting expertise," Lou said.

"Oh, no, they're just a way to *help* us," Heather replied, quick to explain that humans remained in control. "A machine is only as good as what we put into it."

"Yeah, I heard that years ago," Lou replied. "You could probably design a program to analyze data, enter suspects, motives, and other findings and solve the crime in a matter of seconds."

"Well, I may accept that challenge someday, and you may be right."

The doors to the commercial building remained closed and the area cordoned off. Fair officials did not want gawkers walking by the murder scene and craning their necks to see where the body had been found. However, as often happens, people began to leave notes of sympathy at the edge of the barricaded area closest to the Republican booth. Lou, returning to the fairgrounds with Maggie, stopped by every few hours to look over the notes and gifts. All except one mourned the loss of a life by violent means. The note that seemed out of place read, "Do unto others as you would have them do unto you! My husband's killer is free today because of you! May you suffer the fires of eternal damnation!"

Lou lifted the note from the collection with a pair of tweezers and put it in a plastic evidence bag. Then he called Jack on his cell phone.

Jack was enthusiastic. "I've been researching Judge Breckinridge on the Internet. Tell me what more you need and it's as good as done!"

"I need you to review cases that Judge Breckinridge heard. Find any in which a defendant, accused of murdering a married man, was found 'not guilty' by the jury; then, check to see if the judge failed to set aside that verdict when it was obvious to all that the man was guilty. I need the name, address, and phone number of anyone that fits this description."

"You'll request permission for me to review court records?" Jack asked.

"You'll have it by the time you arrive at the courthouse."

three

At the Ingham County Courthouse in downtown Mason, Jack noted a couple of national media trucks in the parking lot. In Judge Winston Breckinridge's anteroom several vases of flowers from friends and colleagues were displayed. Elizabeth Andrews, Judge Breckinridge's secretary, who obviously had been told of Jack's pending arrival, greeted him and provided what he needed.

"Mr. Kelly?" Elizabeth asked.

Jack nodded. "You may use the clerk's office. In addition, two court workers are identifying past murder cases, so you don't need to do that, at least initially."

"Thank you."

"Would you like some coffee?"

"That would be great. Thanks!"

"Cream or sugar, decaf or regular? Or I can send a staff member across the street for a cappuccino if you'd like."

"Regular coffee, black would be fine."

As Elizabeth led Jack to the clerk's office where he could work uninterrupted, a professionally-dressed, middle-aged woman with prematurely-grey hair stopped him by touching his arm.

"Mr. Kelly, may I have a word with you?"

"Certainly," Jack replied.

"In private, please."

"Oh, of course, come in and tell me what's on your mind."

Jack closed the door and offered the woman a chair.

"Thanks for letting me talk to you, Mr. Kelly," she said, sitting at the conference table.

"Is something bothering you? Can you tell me your name first?"

"I'm Cindy Markle. I think I know who killed Judge Breckinridge, and I want to help you and Mr. Searing solve the case."

Jack was so surprised he could only nod.

"I've been a court recorder for eighteen months or so, and I've heard and seen more than most who are familiar with court proceedings in our county. Believe me, I could write a book."

"Yes, I imagine you could."

"I'll be embarrassed if I'm wrong, but I'm convinced the judge was having an affair with a local attorney."

"That's a pretty strong allegation," Jack replied. He took out a pen and his notebook.

"Yes, I know. About a month ago, I returned to the office after regular hours to catch up on filing transcripts. The judge didn't know I was here. I saw and heard the judge and attorney MeLissa Evans alone in his chambers, and let's just say he wasn't hearing a plea bargain. I know that he spent a lot of time in his chambers at night, and MeLissa joined him regularly. I was the only one who came in after hours. I had a key, but I usually told the judge when I was coming into work. I would have told him the night I discovered the inappropriate rendezvous, but it was a spur-of-the-moment decision to return to work. Besides, I thought the judge was attending a Lugnuts game that night. He *never* misses a game when the Lugnuts are in town. Or rather, he never *did*."

"The Lugnuts?" Jack asked, confused.

"A minor-league baseball team, owned by the Toronto Bluejays."

"I see." Jack made another note, then paused to ask Cindy, "How do you spell MeLissa's name?"

"I think it's capital *m* small *a* capital *l* and then small *i-s-s-a*," Cindy replied.

"Assuming you correctly interpreted what you saw and heard, who would want the judge dead?" Jack asked.

"MeLissa's husband."

"Because?"

"Because he's a jealous man, and he has violent tendencies."

"I see," Jack replied. "Could it have been MeLissa herself?"

"I suppose so. Nothing shocks me anymore."

"How about the judge's wife?" Jack asked. "Maybe she knows what you know."

"Actually, she does. I met her coming into the judge's office as I left one afternoon and I told her. I thought she should know about her husband's behavior."

Jack continued with possible suspects. "Or, the murderer might have been a lawyer who lost a case. Or a criminal who believes he or she was judged wrongly."

"I thought I had the answer, Mr. Kelly," Cindy replied, staring at the carpeted floor.

"You might have. But I'm certain that there are many other motives for killing a man."

"I guess you're right. Thanks for listening to me." Cindy rose and moved toward the office door. "I'll let you do the work you came here to do."

"Don't get me wrong, I appreciate your theory," Jack assured her. "We'll check it out, and you may well have solved the case."

"I hope so. Maybe what I've shared will help."

"Any information is good," Jack replied. "But, on another subject, do you recall a murder trial in Judge Breckinridge's court where a man was found 'not guilty' because the judge didn't intervene when it was obvious to everybody in the courtroom that the defendant was guilty?"

Without hesitation, Cindy said, "*The People of Ingham County vs. Thompson.*"

"Okay, thanks." Jack made another note. "I'll look it up."

"It was an ugly case. I'm surprised the judge wasn't featured in a 'That's Ridiculous' *Reader's Digest* column. He sure messed up that case, Mr. Kelly. I don't know why he wasn't disbarred after that fiasco."

"You've really got me curious now."

"It was an interesting case," Cindy replied. "I thought it might make a good movie. It's as good as any story John Grisham could tell!"

"Okay, I'll read that case file first. I trust you'll answer any questions afterwards?" Jack asked.

Cindy nodded. "Sure. But before I go, would you mind if I left some literature from my church with you?"

"I go to church in Muskegon, but if it's important to you, sure, you may set it down by my briefcase."

"Thank you. Our outreach committee distributes literature to outsiders. I appreciate your taking it."

"Not a problem."

With a hot cup of coffee beside him, Jack read the transcript of *The People of Ingham County vs. Thompson*, occasionally making notations in his notebook. He finished the transcript, pulled his thoughts together, and reported to Lou.

"Bill Thompson was charged with the murder of Derrick Hartmann, a telephone solicitor for a regional company that raised money for disabled veterans. Bill Thompson was a construction worker who was mentally unstable. Two witnesses to the crime testified that Thompson stabbed Hartmann outside a bar following an argument over whose turn it was to use the pool table.

"The prosecutor had a clean case: weapon, motive, suspect, and two credible witnesses to the stabbing. A public defender, assigned by the judge, based his defense on the fact that fingerprints on the murder weapon were not Thompson's; he also proposed there was reasonable doubt, in that the person the witnesses saw might have been someone other than his client. The jury was convinced because it was dark outside the bar, and because the prints taken from the murder weapon were quite clear, but did not belong to Thompson. Their verdict was 'not guilty'.

"The judge had the power and the obligation, according to the prosecutor and the Hartmann family, to set aside the verdict and correct this grievous error in judgment. But, Win allowed the decision to stand. Thompson went free, leaving everyone in the court stunned, including Thompson. He told more than one person afterwards that the court system was a joke, admitting he had killed Hartmann. Thompson responded to the lack of fingerprints on the murder weapon by asking, 'Anyone ever hear of gloves?'

"The prosecutor appealed the decision to the next level of review, but the panel sided with the judge, believing in his power to uphold the jury's verdict. Case closed. A guilty man went free."

Lou patiently listened to Jack's summary. "Good work, Jack. The Hartmann family would certainly have reason for revenge. It must have been frustrating to have a guilty man walk away without paying the price for his crime."

"In support of the judge, from my limited knowledge of law, he really couldn't intervene," Jack explained. "The jury system isn't perfect, but it is what we have in this country. If anyone should feel guilty, it's the prosecutor."

"Yes, I know. We have one upset family, that's for sure. I'll ask Maggie to talk to Mrs. Hartmann. Thanks for this survey, Jack. Be sure and give what you found to Heather so she can put it into our computer program."

Norah Hartmann was a single mom raising two daughters, ages four and seven. Norah was caught in a bind: she wanted a full-time job, but could not afford child care. She had no relatives who could help her raise her daughters. She lived in subsidized housing because the pay from her part-time job at Burger King barely put food on the table for her family. For now, a local Methodist church made sure she had basic necessities. Members also provided some respite services so Norah could spend time on her own away from the stress of raising two small girls, one of whom was autistic.

Maggie contacted Norah and made arrangements to meet her at Applebee's on Okemos Road. Norah looked frail. She wore a simple dress, wore no makeup, and looked tired. With a soft drink for Maggie and a Diet Coke for Norah, the two began their conversation.

"Norah, you know I'm working with Lou Searing, investigating the murder of Judge Breckinridge."

"Yes."

"We've learned he was the judge in the trial of Bill Thompson, who was accused of murdering your husband."

"Yes, he was the judge. He did a terrible thing, Mrs. McMillan."

"We've reviewed the case, and it does appear that a mistake was made. I'm not going to defend him, but I have to believe the jury acted in good conscience and based their decision on the information the attorneys presented."

"Thompson killed Darren. I know that. Darren told me about the terrible things Thompson had said to him. I pleaded with Darren not go to the bar because when the two of them were in one place, there was always trouble."

"I don't imagine you'd be surprised to learn that you're a suspect in the judge's murder," Maggie said, watching for a reaction.

Norah simply shook her head slowly with a blank expression. "I can see someone thinking that, but I'll tell you this: if I were going to kill anyone, it would be Thompson, not the judge," Norah said, her voice rising in anger. "Once Thompson is pushing daises, you knock on my door and you'll have the case wrapped up. Think about it, Mrs. McMillan. Why should I go to prison for life, leaving my kids orphans, for killing a judge? Now, killing *Thompson* is a different story, and as far as I know, he is still alive."

"You make a lot of sense, Norah," Maggie replied. "I'll tell Mr. Searing about our conversation. My guess is he'll agree with your reasoning, but we may have more questions."

"Not a problem," Norah replied offering a faint smile. "I like you. I'll help in any way I can. Thanks for the drink."

While Maggie interviewed Norah, Lou went to the fair office and asked for a floor plan of the South Commercial Building as well as a list of booth assignments in the area where the judge was murdered. The booth between Lou and the Republican Party was assigned to The Pampered Chef. Lou had noticed that they seemed to change workers every couple of hours, which made sense, for that's about as long as someone could comfortably be confined to an eight-foot-by-ten-foot space.

Lou contacted the regional supervisor responsible for setting up the Pampered Chef booth and learned that the person assigned to the last shift on August 8 was Kristen Cook. He called Kristen and arranged to speak with her at her home in Haslett, about fifteen miles northeast of Mason.

When Maggie returned from Okemos, she and Lou went to talk with Kristen. The Cook home was not barrier-free so Maggie could not enter. The three decided to go to Lake Lansing Park, a county park not far from Kristen's home.

Kristen quickly got some cookies and made a container of lemonade, and they rode to the park in Maggie's car. On the way, they exchanged comments about working the fair and the unfortunate events of two evenings before. At the park, the three took a path to a picnic table in the shade. With drinks in paper cups and cookies in hand, Lou began.

"You were in your booth, next to the Republican booth, when the power went out, right?"

"Yes. I was sitting in a chair behind a small card table. I was not busy, just watching the people walking past."

"Did you notice anything out of the ordinary?" Lou asked.

"No, unless you call a strange tattoo out of the ordinary. But, at the fair, it seemed like every second person had a tattoo."

"What was odd about the tattoo?" Lou asked.

"It looked like one of those scales of justice, you know, two plates suspended from a bar by chains. It was on a woman's leg — let's see, it would have been her right leg — above the ankle. "

"Uneven scales of justice," Lou repeated, drawing the image in his notebook.

"Anyway, they were not balanced," Kristen continued. "One side was higher than the other."

"Were there any words with the tattoo?" Lou asked.

"I don't think so; I just recall the unbalanced scales."

"What was the woman doing when you noticed her?"

"She was just looking at literature on display at the Republican booth."

"Was the judge in the booth while she was there?" Lou asked.

"You know, I don't know. I didn't know the judge. I'm an independent and have no interest in the two major parties, so I didn't notice who was there."

"Did anything else that night seem odd?"

"No. I don't recall anything."

"What happened when the power went out?" Lou asked.

"There's not much to say. You were there, too. There was a moaning and groaning — you know, when the lights go out unexpectedly in a public setting, people make surprised sounds. Then I saw some people open their cell phones to get some light. About five minutes after the lights went off a deputy came by and told everyone to leave the building. I threw a clean sheet over my products, grabbed my purse and money box, walked out to my car, and went home."

"Did you hear a shot, or any sound, in your area or around the Republican booth?" Lou asked.

"I didn't hear anything besides people talking, moving about, preparing to leave."

"Thanks for talking with me, Kristen." Lou offered his card. "In case you think of anything else."

"I'll call if I think of anything." The three enjoyed small talk for about ten minutes, not wanting to leave the beauty of a warm summer day in the park. Then they drove Kristen home.

Lou suggested he drive so that Maggie could place a call to Karen Scott, the woman assigned to the Republican booth the night the judge was shot. After Maggie explained the reason for the call, she asked. "You were contacted and told to go to the fair office, is that correct?"

"That's right."

"Do you know who called you?" Maggie asked.

"I was told it was a female voice. She didn't identify herself."

"What exactly did the fair staffer say to you?" Maggie asked.

"She called me on my cell and said I had a call at the fair office. She implied it was important, and I should come right away."

"Why didn't she simply give the caller your cell phone number?"

"Confidentiality, I suppose. I wouldn't want the fair office giving my phone number to a stranger."

"You've a point there. So, you left immediately to go to the fair office?"

"Yes, I told Judge Breckinridge I had to leave for a few minutes, took my purse, and left the booth."

"Did you return after you went to the fair office?" Maggie asked.

"No, I had my belongings with me. A deputy told me that unless I needed a purse or other personal items, I should simply leave because of the power failure in the commercial building."

"Did you recognize anyone standing outside your booth just before you left?"

"No. People were milling about, but I don't recall seeing anyone I knew."

"How are you holding up, Karen?" Maggie asked, compassionately. "Are you afraid for yourself because of this?"

"No, I'm okay, I guess. I'm just glad I wasn't in the booth when the gun was fired."

"Do you have any idea why the judge was murdered, or who could have killed him?"

"I'm a recent volunteer. My husband and I moved here a couple of months ago from Toledo where I was active in the Republican Party.

I liked the activity in Toledo, and I thought helping the Republicans here would be a good way to get to know people. I don't know issues or candidates yet."

"If you think of anything else or come across anything you think I'd want to know, I would appreciate your contacting me," Maggie said, before finishing the phone call.

Jack continued to research Judge Breckinridge's history. He talked to a couple of Win's high school and college friends, who described an egotistical know-it-all. From his youth, Win needed to be in control of things, of people, of whatever was around him. In high school, his control of people was expressed by leadership in a gang. In college, he campaigned to become the fraternity active in charge of pledge classes. In law school, he pushed to become captain of the debate team. As he entered the working world, he sought election to president of whatever board he was asked to serve on in his community. His judgeship was another example of control, and his election to Michigan's Legislature would have further satisfied his need. Except for the gang, his obsession was always expressed in socially-acceptable fashion, but hidden beneath the veneer of service was a psychological need to control others.

One of Win's college friends, Morton Baxter, told Jack, "Win was an enigma. On one hand, he truly was interested in helping people, but on the other hand he seemed to want to hurt them. He seemed happiest when someone was disturbed by his actions — or his lack of action."

"Sounds odd," Jack replied. "Can you give me an example?"

"Yes. He led a campus effort to collect books for Africa," Morton began. "He proved adept at getting people to collect books, box them, and feel good about helping others in the process. But, in an interview for the campus paper, he didn't give credit to the two classmates who did most of the work. He said to me later, 'Sherry and Joanne will be furious they were snubbed. I'll enjoy seeing them angry!'

"I was shocked. I asked him, 'You've a problem with giving credit where it's due?'"

"'That's not it,' Win replied. 'It's more fun to watch what they do or say than to imagine the good the project will do.'"

"I said, 'You are sick, Winston!'"

"'It's what it is,'" he replied.

"So, what did the two students do?" Jack asked.

"They wanted revenge. What would you do if you were slighted after working so hard?" Morton asked.

"I'd feel an injustice had been done, but I don't think I'd seek revenge. What did *they* do?"

"They wrote a scathing letter to the campus editor clarifying who did what and where credit should have gone."

"Doesn't sound like revenge to me."

"How about two guys from the college wrestling team taking Win from his dorm in the middle of the night, driving him to the Grand River, stripping him, throwing him in, and taking his clothes as they drove away?" Morton said, chuckling as he recalled the incident.

"Now *that's* revenge!" Jack replied, grinning.

"Big-time!" Morton was grinning, too.

"And you tell me he liked that?" Jack asked, shaking his head.

"He sure did. As I said, he was a sick guy, but, different strokes for different folks."

"I'm almost afraid to ask if you have any other recollections that might help us with this case," Jack replied.

"He was a serious member of the campus Republicans," Morton added.

"And, I assume this 'sick guy', as you refer to him, did something immature?"

"Not really. He seemed to cross the line now and then, but in the political world, it's probably nothing to be concerned about."

"You must have remembered something, or you wouldn't have mentioned it."

"Well, as I said, winning wasn't as important to him as seeing his opponent suffer. That seemed to bring him more joy."

"For example?" Jack asked.

"When the elder Bush won, Winston led an effort to deface the Students for Democrats campus office."

"Why, if the Republicans had already won?" Jack asked.

"Precisely my point," Morton replied. "The election victory was the opportunity to bring on the pain, to rub it in."

"Did the Student Democrats find out who had led the action against their office?"

"It was never officially determined, but they had a pretty good idea. Winston later told us that the leader of the Students for Democrats was a wimp. Anyone worthy of his salt would have whipped him good, he said, almost like he wished the guy had roughed him up."

"I'm no psychiatrist, but this guy sounds masochistic to me," Jack added.

"I don't know if there's a label, but *something* wasn't right with Winston."

four

While Win's body lay on a cold metal slab in Sparrow Hospital, preparations were being made for his funeral. Since Bonnie Breckinridge had no interest in planning a funeral, her best friend, Nicki Nelson, was in Bonnie's home to plan a dignified ceremony. Nicki contacted St. Mary Cathedral in Lansing and spoke with Father McKenzie.

"I'm calling about funeral and burial arrangements for Judge Winston Breckinridge."

"I'm not sure our involvement is possible, Miss Nelson," replied Father McKenzie.

"Not possible? What do you mean?" Vicki replied, surprised at Father's reaction to her request.

"Winston Breckinridge was not a practicing Catholic and, consequently, he's not in good standing with the church."

"What's *that* supposed to mean?" Nicki asked. She was Presbyterian; the idea made no sense to her whatsoever.

"Miss Nelson, it is not appropriate for me to discuss the state of Winston's soul with someone outside the family."

"Fine, then. Tell Bonnie."

"Bonnie knows full well of what I speak," Father McKenzie replied calmly.

"Then, will you officiate at a private service wherever we decide to hold one?" Nicki asked.

"I'm afraid that will not be possible, either."

Nicki thanked the Father for talking with her and ended the conversation.

Next, Nicki called Gorsline-Runciman Funeral Home in East Lansing about holding a service there.

"Mrs. Nelson, we would be pleased to have Judge Breckinridge's service at our home. But his notarized orders on file here state he wished to be cremated and that no service be held."

"Nonsense! Hundreds of people will want to pay their respects. We need to hold a funeral."

"Mrs. Nelson, we respect the wishes of our clients. We'll hold no service here. I'm sorry."

Exasperated, Nicki called Win's good friend and colleague in Ingham County, Judge Buikema, and explained her predicament.

"I wouldn't try to do anything, Nicki," Judge Buikema responded after a moment. "I'm not sure he would want a service."

"But, *everybody* should have a service!" Nicki retorted.

"No, *not* everyone has a service. While a funeral may normally be expected, Win may have chosen not to have one.

"*Why*, for Heaven's sake?"

"There are a number of reasons," Judge Buikema explained. "The person may have decided not to offer the opportunity for people to say things publicly that might be embarrassing. Or, someone may fear that nobody would come."

"What difference does it make? He's dead!" Nicki sputtered, frustrated with hitting roadblocks.

"It might not make a difference to him, but if few people want to honor the man, even when he's dead, it might be difficult for his children or friends to swallow."

"I don't get it. The man was a prominent judge, and a candidate for the Legislature."

"That sounds admirable to some, but to others it may not."

"So, you think we should just have the man cremated and forget it," Nicki summarized.

"Evidently it's what he wanted," Judge Buikema replied. "If I were you, I would simply invite friends and acquaintances to some type of get-together where they can share memories."

Nicki sighed. "Okay, I guess that's what we'll do. There doesn't appear to be any other choice. Thank you, Judge."

Nicki explained to Bonnie what she had done and what Judge Buikema had advised.

Bonnie was adamant. "Nicki, I don't want anything to do with it. I don't want to sit around with his friends listening to good-old-boy stories. The man is no longer on the earth. I'm done. *Forget* it."

"People will wonder if you don't have an event of some kind to honor your husband."

"I don't care what other people think," Bonnie replied. "I've never cared, and I'm not going to begin caring now."

"So, have him cremated, and then we spread his ashes some-where?" Nicki suggested, resigned to a minimal remembrance.

Bonnie shook her head. "No, we won't spread his ashes." Bonnie's expression brightened. "He's leaving plenty of money behind, though. I'll buy a plot in a cemetery, buy him a big headstone he would be proud of, and put the ashes in the plot."

"You'll get two plots, so you can join him?" Nicki asked hopefully.

Bonnie smiled at her friend. "Ah, no, Nicki. Win loved his whippet, Skinny. We'll take her ashes from the mantel and lay them beside him for company."

"I'm sorry. I just don't understand all of this," Nicki replied, throwing up her hands in frustration.

"Well, adjust to it, Nicki. This is over, honey, O-V-E-R. I don't want to hear another word."

"But — what about the obituary? He was a prominent citizen. He deserves a nice write-up in the *Lansing State Journal*," Nicki said.

"Winston Breckinridge was born, judged, and died. Short, and to the point."

"But…"

"*Enough*, Nicki," Bonnie interrupted. "Let me know when you want to talk about something other than my former husband. Am I understood?"

"But — okay."

"Now, if you'll excuse me, I'm going to dinner with a gentleman."

"A date?" Nicki asked, very surprised with what she'd just heard.

"Call it what you will. I call it dinner with a friend."

The phone rang. "Get that, will you, Nicki? I don't want to talk to anyone." Bonnie rose and headed for the stairs.

"Hello, Breckinridge residence."

"Nicki, is that you?" a woman asked in a tenuous voice.

"Yes. How's it going?"

"I called to talk to Bonnie, but actually I'd rather talk to you."

"Okay."

"I made a huge mistake the night of Win's murder. I forgot about my tattoo and I didn't wear slacks. If somebody saw me at the booth before the murder, I could have some explaining to do."

"Okay. But why are you telling me this?"

"If you hear anything about the police looking for a woman with a tattoo, would you let me know?"

"I don't know how I'd hear; but, sure."

"Thanks, Nicki." The woman sounded relieved.

"So, do you want to talk to Bonnie?"

"No, tell her Hi, is all."

Nicki put the phone down on its cradle and stepped to the bottom of the stairs. She shouted, "Bonnie? That was Artie. She says Hi."

The August 10th edition of the *Lansing State Journal* contained a death notice. It read:

> *Ingham County Judge Winston Breckinridge, age 45, of East Lansing, Michigan, died August 8. There will be no service. Arrangements are being handled by the East Lansing Gorsline-Runciman Funeral Home.*

Wednesday afternoon, Lou, Jack, Maggie, and Heather met at the Comfort Inn to strategize and to summarize what they had learned. Everyone but Jack decided to stay overnight. Jack had commitments in Muskegon, and he felt he could do whatever was needed from his home by computer and phone.

After dinner, the three decided to get their minds off the murder. Lou was able to get tickets to *The Lion King* being performed at Michigan State University's Wharton Center. The show was phenomenal, and they thoroughly enjoyed it. On the way back to their motel, they decided to meet in the lobby for breakfast.

five

During the early-morning exercise period, two of the trustees who had worked the fair met on the basketball court on the grounds of the county jail.

"You found the guy's body, huh?" Bob asked, a cigarette dangling from his lips as he bounced a slightly-deflated basketball.

"Deader than a doornail," Randy Pollard replied.

"What did you do?" Bob asked.

"What did I do? Did I talk to him and invite him to play poker with us?" Randy said chuckling. "I went to Bud and told him what I found."

Bob grinned. "Hey! The guy was the judge who sent you up, wasn't he?"

"Yeah, he sent me up, but I didn't kill him."

"Then you were in on the plan, I'll bet. Right?" Bob asked, dribbling the ball around his back, trying to tease a confession from his buddy.

"No, I wasn't. I didn't have anything to do with it."

"Cops been here to talk to you yet?" Bob asked.

"No," Randy said, not wanting to admit to talking with a deputy at the command center after he found the body.

"Well, they *will* be."

"What makes you think so?" Randy asked.

"Are you crazy, man?" Bob asked. "You find the guy dead, the same guy who sentenced you to this godforsaken place. Working the fair was an opportunity for revenge, and you took advantage of it. You look guilty as they come."

"I *said*, I didn't have anything to *do* with it!"

"Well, nobody's going to believe that, man. You better find a good lawyer."

"You think so?" Randy asked, realizing this didn't look good for him. "I only know the lawyer who represented me at the trial, and I haven't got a penny to pay her, anyway."

"You can plan on leaving here and going to prison."

"But, I didn't *do* anything to that guy!" Randy's frustration was obvious.

"Play this out, Randy. We got in the van back to the jail at 11:15 p.m., but the guy was shot when the breaker box blew around eleven. Someone on the outside brought a gun with a silencer into the fairgrounds and hid it where you could get it. You popped the guy, and you find him in the morning because you know he's dead. You figure people won't think you did it because you're the good guy finding the body. You put the gun back where your outside friend hid it, and he takes it home to bury or do whatever he can to keep it from being an issue. The judge is dead, and you look innocent, but in reality, you got away with murder."

"You really think I'll get the rap for this?" Randy asked.

"I not only *think* it, I *know* it," Bob replied. "You should've let someone else find the guy, Randy. That was your mistake." Bob tossed the ball through the net, proud of himself for describing what probably happened at the fair the night of August 8.

Lou suggested that Maggie observe Win Breckinridge's autopsy at Sparrow Hospital in Lansing. He made arrangements with Leon Abbott, the hospital administrator responsible for the Autopsy Unit, for Maggie to meet with the pathologist who would oversee the judge's autopsy.

Maggie was a bit apprehensive; she had never been in a morgue before, much less seen an autopsy. She exited her car, retrieved her chair, then wheeled herself into the hospital and on to the Autopsy Unit. Several people waited in the reception area, perhaps preparing themselves to identify a loved one.

Leon greeted Maggie and escorted her into the working area of the office. He introduced her to the pathologist, Dr. Oscar Leonard, who was studying the judge's file when Maggie arrived.

"Thank you for meeting with me, Doctor. I hope you can help us understand the cause and manner of Winston's death."

"I think we can help with that. I expect the cause of death was a bullet to the chest which disrupted blood flow. Simply put, the man probably bled to death. I've ordered toxicology tests, and the results will tell us whether drugs or alcohol played any part in his death."

"I see," Maggie replied. "What do you anticipate was the manner of death?"

"Homicide. It was not an accident, and it was not a suicide — unless he hired someone to shoot him, which is highly unlikely."

"Did you find the bullet?" Maggie asked.

"Yes, and an x-ray confirmed that it's lodged in the chest. It damaged the ribs; and a combination of lung, muscle, and bone kept the projectile within the body,"

"What happens after the autopsy?" Maggie asked.

"A funeral home will take the body and prepare it for cremation or burial. We'll file our report with the sheriff who must determine whether a criminal act was committed, and if so, by whom."

"You have a pretty smooth system," Maggie said, impressed with the efficiency and thoroughness of the procedures.

"Well, we need to be efficient, given the number of bodies that come through here."

"I understand that, by law, you must perform autopsies on a variety of victims?"

"Yes, all children must be autopsied. Any adult who wasn't seen by a doctor within 48 hours of his or her death must be autopsied. Any suspicious deaths mandate the procedure, and of course, suspected suicide or homicide."

"Thank you. May I receive a copy of your report?"

"Not directly. Either a judge must release the report to you or Sheriff Lloyd will provide a copy."

"Thank you for your time." Maggie left without witnessing the autopsy, which was fine with her. She would meet Lou following his interview with Randy Pollard, and then she and Heather would head home.

Mid-morning, Lou Searing walked into the Ingham County Jail off Cedar Street, on the west side of Mason and introduced himself to the deputy at the desk. "I'm here to talk to Randy Pollard."

"One minute, please, Mr. Searing."

In about five minutes, Lou was escorted through several locked doors into what appeared to be an interrogation room. Inside, a guard stood against the back wall while Randy Pollard, a slightly-built man about 25 years old, sporting tattoos on both arms, sat at a table. He had a full head of hair, neatly combed. Despite the orange jumpsuit, he was a handsome man.

"Mr. Pollard, my name is Lou Searing. I'm investigating the murder of Judge Breckinridge." Randy simply nodded and turned his eyes to the floor.

"I realize you have talked with the state police, but I have a few questions of my own." Randy continued to look down.

"I understand you found the judge's body in the South Commercial Building on the fairgrounds. Is that correct?" Randy nodded again.

"Did you know the judge? Did you have any dealings with him?" Lou asked.

Randy looked up. "Can I have a lawyer?"

"We can arrange that. A little nervous, are you?"

"Yeah."

"Do you have a lawyer?" Lou asked.

"A public defender was assigned to me, but I don't remember her name."

"The sheriff has it on file. I'll find it." At the front desk, Lou learned the attorney assigned to Randy was an acquaintance, Tracy Boxer. He called her and explained that he wanted to ask general questions of Pollard. She would come to the jail immediately. Conveniently, her office was located in Holt, a town near Mason, so Lou waited twenty minutes until she arrived. Before going back into the interrogation room, Lou and Tracy spoke briefly.

"You know better than to interview my client without my permission," Tracy chastised Lou.

"I'm just asking basic questions," Lou replied. "He asked for you right away."

"In answering a basic question, he might provide incriminating information. You guys are pretty good with those 'Have you stopped beating your wife?' questions."

"You know me better than that, Tracy."

"I trust you, Lou — you're right on that — but you know I never want you talking to a client without my knowledge."

"I apologize. When I asked him if he was the one who found the judge the morning of August 8, he nodded. I asked if he knew the judge, and he asked for his lawyer."

"No harm done then. Let's get this over with," Tracy said.

The two entered the room. Attorney Boxer greeted Randy and sat down beside him. He seemed relieved that Tracy was there.

Lou spoke. "Randy, I believe my last question was, 'Did you know the judge or have any dealings with him?'"

"He was the judge at my trial."

"Did he do right by you?" Lou asked.

"The jury was convinced I held up the store, so they decided I was guilty."

"The judge sentenced you?"

"Yes."

"A fair sentence?"

"I suppose."

"So, did you feel Judge Breckinridge treated you unfairly?" Lou asked.

"No, the prosecutor did, but not the judge."

"Okay, back to the fair. Did you see or hear anything strange the evening of the murder?" Lou asked.

"One of the guys in my jail detail said he saw somebody in overalls near the commercial building breaker box. He thought it was funny because there was no Consumers Energy truck around. The guy at the box seemed to know what he was doing; but he was alone and Consumers people always work in pairs."

"You said, 'the guy', so the person at the breaker box was a man?" Lou asked.

"I guess he didn't say it was a man. Maybe I assumed that."

"Where is this breaker box?" Lou asked.

"It's an out-of-the-way cabinet at the back of the commercial building." Randy pointed to the location on Lou's plan.

"Who told you all of this, Randy?" Lou asked.

"I can't say. Telling the cops something I heard and then pointing them to the person is a ticket to a lot of trouble. I'll talk to him and see if he'll come forward on his own."

"That's fair," Lou said. "Is there anything else you can help me with?"

"I don't think so."

"Thank you, Mr. Pollard. I appreciate your honesty and your information." Lou started to get out of his chair, but Randy held up his hand to stop him.

"Mr. Searing, I've been in trouble a lot, and I've been questioned by a lot of police detectives. But you are the first person to treat me with respect instead of like a punk. Thank you."

Lou rose, shook Randy's hand, and thanked Attorney Boxer for representing her client. They agreed that they would no doubt be talking again soon.

Heather had completed her computer program for cataloging suspects and information about them. In entering data, she came to see a pattern or two herself. One observation that captured her interest was the obviously unemotional reaction from the judge's wife, Bonnie. Such lack of emotion certainly led Heather to thoughts of a hired killing, if she didn't do it herself.

Risking a reprimand from Lou, Heather decided to seek personal information about Bonnie Breckinridge. She called Bonnie and asked to meet with her, ostensibly because she was taking an art appreciation class at Western Michigan University. Bonnie Breckinridge was a fine artist, well established in the Lansing area.

The meeting took place in the Breckinridge home on Harrison Street in East Lansing, Michigan. Heather drove her accessible van to the Breckinridge estate. The entrance to the home was accessible because Bonnie often entertained several older women who needed a barrier-free entrance to the home. Once inside, Heather noticed that Bonnie's extravagant paintings adorned walls throughout the house. An abstract style and their colorful motif made the work a joy to view and study.

"Mrs. Breckinridge, I have two reasons for meeting with you. I apologize for mentioning only one when I asked to see you," Heather began.

"You want to talk to me about Win's murder, right?" Bonnie was matter-of-fact.

"Yes, that's right."

"Then let's get that out of the way before we talk art. One should always eat the liver and onions before enjoying the strawberry shortcake!" Bonnie smiled and Heather nodded, chuckling in slight embarrassment. Bonnie Breckinridge was an obese woman, forty-four years of age with long, braided hair. "What do you want to know?" Bonnie asked.

"Do you know of anyone who would want to kill your husband?"

"As I told Mr. Searing, there are a lot of people. If I listed them, it would take quite a while to cover everyone."

"So, he was *really* disliked?" Heather asked.

"Honey, he was more than disliked — hated is more accurate."

"Why?" Heather replied. "I mean, most people have someone who despises them, but why so many?"

"Let me put it this way," Bonnie began. "I noticed in the paper that one of the high school students won a recent oratory contest. The title of his talk was 'God is First, the Other Person is Second, and I'm Third.' If Win wrote the speech, the title would be 'I am First, I am Second, and If At All Possible, I am Also Third!'"

"Now, that's a unique title if I ever heard one," Heather replied.

"Well, it's true. Win was a control freak. Those who could further his control he tolerated and they felt accepted, but only on his terms. Everyone else was to be contained, controlled, and dominated."

"Except you…" Heather added.

"Oh, no, including me."

"And that's why you don't feel sad at his death?"

"Exactly. As Martin Luther King said in his, 'I Have a Dream' speech, 'Thank God Almighty, I'm free at last!'"

"Why didn't you just divorce him?" Heather asked, puzzled.

"That's a conversation for another time."

"Did you kill him to get your freedom?" Heather asked.

"I told Mr. Searing, 'Absolutely not,' but to you I will say, I was a party to his death."

"Why would you tell me something contrary to what you told Mr. Searing?"

"You're a woman, Heather."

"But you know I'll talk to Mr. Searing."

"You do what you need to do. I respect that."

"What does 'a party to his death' mean?" Heather repeated.

"It means I provided information about him."

"To someone you expected to kill him?"

"Yes."

"Did you hire someone?" Heather asked, astounded.

"Heather, it's time to talk about my art. What is it about my style and technique that you'd like to discuss?"

The next hour was delightful; Heather enjoyed Bonnie's art and learned much about the masters of the Romantic Period. After their discussion and a chat over hot tea and crumpets, Heather excused herself and returned to her motel.

six

Lou was in Grand Haven preparing for his Knights of Columbus meeting at St. Patrick's Catholic Church. He was the recorder, so the pencils were sharpened and the minutes were up-to-date.

Lou backed his Harley out of the garage for the seven-mile trip to the church. He greeted his brother Knights and prepared his materials for the meeting. After the opening ceremonies were complete, Lou's cell phone rang. He was embarrassed, silenced it quickly, and glanced at the display. Lou figured Jack could wait, so he turned off the phone, apologized, and returned his full attention to the meeting.

Jack was puzzled; Lou always answered his phone. Jack couldn't leave a message, and he knew the phone was off because it had only rung twice. Negative thoughts came into his mind, but then he realized Lou could be momentarily occupied with something more important.

An hour later, Lou returned the call. He explained why he had turned off the phone, and he appreciated Jack's concern for his welfare.

"So, what do you have, Jack?" Lou asked.

"A new suspect."

"At this stage of the game, a new suspect is par for the course."

"This one is a bit different. He's not a Democrat, a victim of a bad court decision, an attorney, is not even involved with the fair. One guess is all you get, Lou."

"Whoever the judge beat in the primary election," Lou offered. "The killer is a jealous Republican taking his or her frustration out on a fellow Republican."

"What have you got against Republicans, Lou?" Jack asked.

"Nothing. My parents and some of my best friends are misdirected is all."

"I suppose you're a Democrat?" Jack asked.

"I consider the candidate, whoever I think will do the best job. I vote across the political spectrum."

"Even a communist or a Libertarian?"

"I must admit I've not voted for a communist, but a Libertarian or two has slipped into the voting booth and whispered in my ear."

"A bit off-topic, but an interesting aspect of your life, Lou."

"I give up; who's the suspect?" Lou asked.

"Zippy Roelof. He was responsible for a ride named the Egg-Beater, one of those rides that spins while going up and down."

"So, we're back at the fair?" Lou asked.

"In a way, but not the *Ingham* County Fair. Zippy was fired about a year ago from his job with a carnival company. A woman was flung out of the ride, allegedly because the safety bar wasn't secure across her lap. Zippy was found to be negligent as he was to check each bar before the capsule went spinning around."

"What does this have to do with the judge?"

"Judge Breckinridge presided at Zippy's trial. The defense attorney claimed the woman was dead at the time of the accident; therefore, Zippy was not responsible, and he should not have been tried for her death."

"How could she die before being flung from the ride?" Lou asked.

"Her toxicology report demonstrated that her body was so full of drugs, the pathologist admitted he was surprised she was able to climb the steps to the ride, much less get into the Egg-Beater capsule, or whatever those metal shells are called.

"The judge ruled that, because the medical examiner could not verify the woman died prior to the accident, Mr. Roelof should be tried for negligent homicide. Zippy was convicted and is being held in the Thumb Correctional Facility in Lapeer."

"How can Zippy be a suspect in the judge's murder?" Lou asked.

"He developed a friendship with another Lapeer prisoner, Denny Daly, who became obsessed with Zippy's case. Daly promised to avenge Zippy when he got out. Daly was released five days before the judge's murder."

"Doesn't look good for the guy," Lou remarked. "Denny Daly, right? How did you learn all of this, Jack?"

"A third prisoner in Lapeer knew of the tie between Zippy and Denny, but he didn't like Denny. I guess the guy was stealing his cigarettes. Anyway, I got a call from this third party, Henry Posse, who told me the whole story."

"This Henry didn't know Denny actually killed the judge, did he?" Lou asked.

"No. He just told me about them and figured we should know that maybe Denny killed the judge for Zippy."

"Thanks, Jack. Good work!"

Early on Friday, August 12, Lou called the Correctional Facilities Administration and talked to Tony Sisco, the manager responsible for prisoner data.

"Tony, Lou Searing here. I'm working on the Judge Breckinridge murder in Ingham County, and I need some information."

"If I have it, it's yours, Lou."

"A man named Denny Daly was released about a week ago. I need to know his address and the nature of the crime that put him in Lapeer."

"I'm sitting at my computer, so I'll have it in a second. Okay, the address he provided at the time of his release is Imlay City. He served six years, two months, and four days for armed robbery and as an accomplice to a murder in Flint."

"Could he be armed and dangerous?"

"Apparently he was a model prisoner. He earned his GED and then completed our prisoner reentry program, meaning he now has skills for jobs available to him. He has a place to live, and the parole supervisor expects him to be an example of how our new prisoner reentry initiative works. You suspect him of something, Lou?"

"Apparently he befriended a man named Zippy Roelof in the Thumb Facility. Word is, he had a lot of sympathy for Zippy, who had a major beef with Judge Breckinridge. So, we're wondering if Daly could have killed the judge for his buddy."

"Anything is possible, but that doesn't sound like Denny. Let me know what happens and call if you need anything more."

"Thanks, Tony," Lou said. "Oh, one more thing. What can you tell me about Henry Posse?"

"Let me pull him up. He's also in Lapeer. He was convicted of murder, sentenced in Detroit on August 14th of 2004. The notes from his intake evaluation say Henry is arrogant, cocky, blames the world for everything bad that has happened to him. We might expect trouble with inmates in his cell block, so he's closely monitored. Is he in trouble, too?" Tony asked.

"He's our informant at the moment."

"Take it all with a grain of salt, Lou."

"Yeah, we will, but you never know — the guy could be right on the money with this one."

"Good luck, Lou. Regards to Jack and Maggie."

seven

FRIDAY EVENING, AUGUST 12TH
GRAND HAVEN, MICHIGAN

Lou was raised in Grand Haven and knew the dangers of living in a lakeside community. People are washed off the pier when waves are high. Kids are pulled out into the lake by undertows, and sometimes they drown. Boating accidents occur on perfect days, when the beach is crowded with tourists. Because of these dangers, children are lectured and monitored closely, but at the same time offered the chance to enjoy the water and what nature has provided.

Lou and Carol's four grandchildren from Grand Rapids, and four more from St. Louis, Missouri, spend summer vacations at the Searing home. The grandchildren range in age from twelve to two. Before each child is allowed in Lake Michigan, he or she has passed a swimming test and understands about undertows and how to escape them. The children love the waves: "The bigger, the better!" they exclaim. But they know that danger comes with the fun, and anyone who acts recklessly is called back to shore and denied the Lake for a period of time.

When the evening weather is suitable, Lou and Carol stroll along the water's edge. It's a special time for both because there are no interruptions. It's also a chance for Carol to catch up on Lou's current investigation.

"Any leads in the judge's murder at the county fair?" Carol asked. She hoped the case would be resolved soon because, while she supported Lou's investigations, she would prefer he take on a less hazardous hobby.

"We've suspects, but no one stands out."

"As I recall, the judge seemed to foster controversy wherever he went," Carol replied.

"That's what we hear. I have yet to find someone who has only good things to say about the man. But a judge deals with conflict, so having people upset with him comes with the territory."

"How is his wife handling his death?" Carol asked.

"She seems to be happy as a June bug!" Lou replied with a chuckle.

"Really?"

"We think they had been estranged for some time."

"Still, isn't it a bit odd to be happy at someone's death?" Carol asked. "Sounds like she might move a bit higher on your list of suspects."

"She's up there, all right." Lou's cell phone rang. The number displayed was Maggie's, and once again, he decided he could call back. The walk was not to be interrupted. This was a special, quiet time in nature. Carol and Lou decided to turn around and return to their home. Soon they saw Samm standing on the porch, her tail wagging, anticipating petting and a brushing.

From his home office, Lou called Maggie. "Hope your message wasn't critical. Carol and I were out on the shore when you called. What's up?"

"I wanted you to know that tomorrow is Heather's twenty-first birthday. She doesn't want to draw attention, but I thought you might like to help her celebrate in some way."

"Thanks for telling me. Carol will know what I should do."

"Anything major happening on your end?"

"Nothing. The big news of the day is Heather turning 21."

Early on Saturday, August 13, Lou thought to call Lester Grant, the judge's opponent in the upcoming election. Despite assurances that Lester Grant would not kill anyone, Lou needed to interview him to form his own opinion. A phone call should be sufficient for this first meeting, he thought. Lester answered the call as he sat in a restaurant in Lansing.

After introducing himself, Lou began, "My sources tell me that you could be considered a suspect in the murder of Judge Breckinridge."

"I don't doubt it for a minute," Lester replied. "Political campaigns are notorious for back-stabbing and putting one's self in a good light while discrediting your opponent. I've been in several elections, so I know the ropes and play the game within my ethical and moral limits."

"You seem to have a solid grasp of the process," Lou said.

"I'd like to think so."

"Have you any idea who could have killed the judge?" Lou asked.

"Well, I've given that a lot of thought, and I have my list of possibilities."

"Please give me your list," Lou responded.

"First of all, I truly do not believe it was anyone in the political world because we all understand campaigning. Having said that, I understand you might think I killed Judge Breckinridge, being his opponent and all. But I think you'd be wasting your time pursuing people in either the Democratic or Republican parties. High on my list would be Bonnie. She wouldn't surprise me — very odd couple, they seemed to detest one another. Family aside, how about attorney

MeLissa Evans' husband? I've heard rumors of affairs for more than a year, so I could see him having reason to kill the judge.

"But, here's one you haven't heard, I'll bet," Les continued. "Judge Breckinridge was playing golf in a foursome at the Walnut Hills Country Club a couple of years ago, and well, you aren't going to believe this. I'm not sure I do, but the judge supposedly made a hole-in-one. As you may know, to be a legitimate ace it must be witnessed, and it was. Except, one of the players refused to confirm it, and the club pro wouldn't accept the shot as a hole-in-one."

"I'm a golfer, so I understand that world," Lou replied, always eager for a golf story. "Tell me about this episode."

"The ball came down and stuck into the lip of the cup. It didn't fall *into* the cup. The pin was removed, but the ball still wouldn't fall. The ball looked like it could fall any second, as if gravity would surely drop it, but it didn't. The foursome waited about five minutes, but it didn't fall. They had to move along, so Judge Win removed the ball and repaired the mark made on the lip of the cup. The judge declared it a hole-in-one, and two others agreed, but the fourth guy said, 'Absolutely not!' The ball needed to fall into the cup to be a hole-in-one; if that didn't happen, and it hadn't, then it was *not* a hole-in-one. So, he wouldn't attest to it.

"The judge went berserk — he was furious! I guess the judge threatened the guy, saying he would bring him down. What 'bring him down' meant was not clear, but the judge had lost it emotionally. Maybe the guy who wouldn't agree had felt enough stress and decided to solve the problem by getting rid of the judge."

"Could be. Who is the guy? Do you know?" Lou asked.

"Yes, but I don't want word to get out that I think he killed the judge. I am simply telling you about a confrontation."

"That's not a problem."

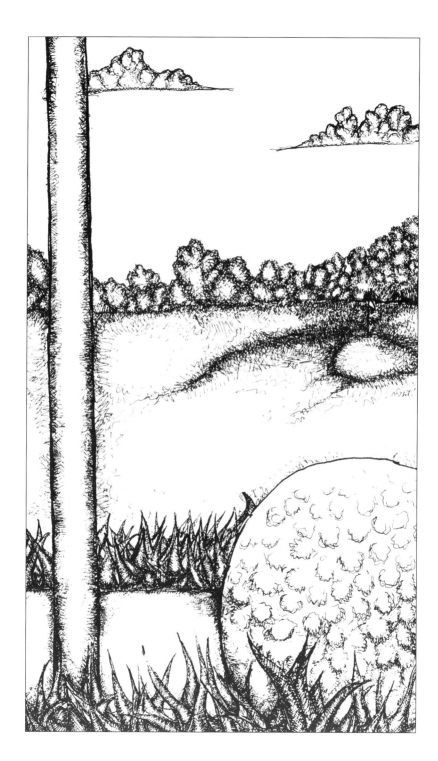

"His name's Colon Manley. He owns a hunting supply store in Perry."

Lou wrote the name down. "Is anyone else on your list?"

"Yes, one more — Wilma Simmons. Wilma is quite a character. She used to be a domestic, I think you call them. Now, she heads a union of domestics. She's very good at what she does, and she's hired by the Who's Who in Lansing and Flint. She's been known to do favors for many of her clients. These favors are often not legal, but she does them anyway."

"Example?" Lou asked.

"Usually extortion, black mail kinds of things."

"I don't understand."

"Well, say one of her clients wants to start a rumor," Les began. "For the right amount of money, Wilma will plant the rumor in the right place and let it grow. Some of the rumors have been damaging. Some people are even convinced she committed arson a while back. Rumor has it that she sent the old Traverse Hotel up in flames a year ago."

"That was a huge blaze," Lou replied.

"Yes, well, she supposedly set it, or arranged to have it set, either for revenge for a client, or for insurance money, or whatever."

"I see."

"So I can see her arranging the murder of the judge, if someone was willing to pay her to do it right."

"OK. Is anyone else on your list?" Lou asked.

"No, that's about it. Any other questions for me?" Lester asked.

"Just one," Lou said. He paused, then asked, "Did you kill the judge?"

"I can't believe you would ask such a thing!" Les sputtered.

"Does your meeting with Wilma a week before the murder give credence to my question?"

"This conversation is finished!" Lester hissed as he turned off his phone.

Jack had reported to Lou that Lester Grant had talked with Wilma Simmons a week before the murder, when they discussed what Grant could do to receive the endorsement of the Association of Domestic Workers (ADW). Jack had obtained a list of organizations endorsing Grant for State Representative, as well as a list of contacts Grant had made in seeking the endorsement. Each endorsement included the name and number of the person giving permission to publish their organizational name in a list soon to appear in the State Journal.

During lunch on Saturday it occurred to Lou how the 4-H group from Rives Junction could help with the investigation. He contacted Lisa Myers and learned that a club meeting was to be held that evening. Lou was invited to use a speaker phone to share his ideas with the club.

Just before calling the 4-H group, Lou took a call from attorney Tracy Boxer.

"Hi, Tracy. What can I do for you?"

"I've talked with Randy Pollard. He has decided not to ask a fellow inmate to talk to you about seeing someone near the breaker box."

"That's fine. I appreciate your getting back to me."

Mrs. Myers talked with her 4-H group about a rare and great opportunity. She explained to the members that they may be able to assist Mr. Searing in solving a crime. A few of the club members had read Lou's books and were familiar with his investigations. At the agreed-upon-hour, Lou called Lisa and after an introduction, he began.

"Mrs. Myers tells me that you are willing to help us. Perhaps she committed you to something already?"

"We want to help, Mr. Searing. I'm Becky Smith, club president. How many kids get to work with a detective? Not many. We look forward to helping you."

"All right then. First, you need to understand that what I'll ask you to do is not exciting. There will be no pursuing of criminals, no gunfire, no car chases with red and blue lights flashing. Your assistance will simply involve tasks to be taken seriously and searches for information that might help the case."

"Mr. Searing, my name is Larry Billings. What do you need?"

"I need you to conduct an experiment, probably in conjunction with professors at Michigan State University. An incident related to the case I am working on concerns the death of someone, allegedly because of a carnival ride, but, the woman may have died before the ride began. During the ride on the Egg-Beater, her body was flung out of the capsule. Are you all familiar with this ride?"

Mrs. Myers said, "Several heads are nodding, Lou."

"Good. When the ride was stopped and help arrived, the woman was dead. The question in court was whether the woman was dead before she fell from the ride or falling out of the ride killed her.

"So, in the course of this experiment, I need to learn what force would cause the security bar that goes across the rider's lap to give way. I can arrange for access to an Egg-Beater capsule, and I can tell you the rider weighed three hundred fifty pounds. You will need to understand the physics involved, because the issue is what it takes to restrain an object, dead or alive, from breaking through the security bar while other forces act on the body."

"I understand the ride operator was tried for negligent homicide on the assumption that the security bar either malfunctioned or hadn't sufficient strength to keep the rider inside the capsule," Mrs. Myers offered.

"That's correct. The company that makes the Egg-Beater will cooperate and pay any expenses you incur during your research. What do you think? Would you like to take on the project?"

Lou heard several of the members reply in unison, "Yes."

"That's great. Thanks. Mrs. Myers and I will be in touch."

Heather hadn't told Lou about Bonnie Breckinridge's remark that she was a party to her husband's murder. She was afraid Lou would be upset and lecture her for interviewing the judge's wife without his okay. Heather would rather have sent Lou an e-mail, but she needed to face him out of respect. So, she arranged to visit him at home.

A couple of hours later, Heather arrived at Lou's home. She was invited in and the two of them sat in the living room. Lou sensed tension that was uncomfortable. Lou said, "You wanted to talk to me?"

"I feel like a penitent in the confessional because I did something I shouldn't have," Heather began, looking down at the floor. "I know you'll be upset, and I'm ready for your reprimand, even exclusion from this case or any future one."

"Wow, this must be some confession. What on earth did you do?" Lou asked, trying to reassure her.

"I interviewed the judge's wife on my own."

"I see." Lou paused in thought. "Did you learn anything?"

"She said she was a party to the judge's murder."

"Great work, Heather!"

"Great work? I put my nose where it doesn't belong. Aren't you *upset* with me?"

"Yes, I am. You've got to learn — and hopefully you *have* — that solving a murder is a team effort, and we can't work in isolation. But, it appears no harm was done, and you may have learned something important. I'm a bit disappointed but otherwise it's okay. I can give you some leeway as you learn how to investigate, but you're still a bit green. So, for now, tell me what you think should be done, and maybe I'll assign it. That depends on where the case is going."

"Thank you, Mr. Searing. I'm so relieved!"

"Good. I'm glad you came forward. Now, *you* said she was a party to the murder. She told *me* she had nothing to do with it."

"Yes, she told me that. When I asked why she admitted it to me, she said it was because I was a woman."

"What does that mean?" Lou asked.

"I don't know. Maybe later it will all make sense."

"I wonder what 'party to the crime' means?" Lou pondered.

"She spoke of 'information.' I suppose that could be anything from a contract to kill to telling someone where her husband would be that evening," Heather mused.

"We'll add it to the data. Good work, Heather. You got lucky on that one."

"Guess I did. Again, I'm sorry. I've learned my lesson."

eight

Lou remained intrigued by Kristen Cook's description of the leg tattoo on the woman standing near the Republican booth the night of the murder. He drove to Lansing, planning to talk with a tattoo artist. He entered Al's Tattoos and asked to speak to the owner. A man, with what appeared to be 80% of his body covered in embedded ink, came from a back room of the parlor.

"I'm Al. You wanted to see me. What do you need?"

"I've a couple of questions."

"Shoot."

"Do people choose from a catalog for tattoos, or can you make a tattoo from a request?" Lou asked.

"Both. Some people know what they want, describe it to us, and we design the tattoo for their approval. Others aren't sure what they want. Those folks look at a lot of catalogs before asking us to do a design."

"Do you keep records on who gets what tattoo?"

"*I* do, but only because it makes sense in running a business."

"So no law requires you to keep those records," Lou surmised.

"Obviously, I keep financial records for taxes," Al replied. "So, I know who got what tattoo, on what date, and how much they paid for it."

"Do you keep a photo collection of those you do?"

"No."

"If I described a tattoo, would you know whether you provided it to a customer?"

"Probably."

"I'm trying to find out whether anyone requested a tattoo of a scale of justice tipped significantly to one side. Do you know the design I mean?"

"Yes, and the answer is, 'No', I haven't done one like that."

"Thank you," Lou said. "But if you see or hear of a tattoo like that near a woman's right ankle, would you please give me a call? Here's my card."

"Yes."

"Thank you for your time," Lou said, before turning and heading for the door.

Lou wanted to talk to Henry Posse to clarify the informant's story. He drove from Lansing to Lapeer to meet with him. After signing papers and passing through countless locked passageways, Lou found himself in the interview room. Across from him, holding a phone receiver to his ear, was Henry Posse.

"I'm Lou Searing. I suppose I'm your uncle coming to wish you a happy birthday," Lou said, knowing that prisoners who have visitors often need to lie to keep rumors at bay.

"That's right. Word will spread that I had a visitor, and you can bet you're not a private eye, at least not when I'm asked."

"As you know, I'm investigating the murder of Judge Breckinridge," Lou began. "You contacted my associate, Jack Kelly, and told him you think Denny Daly may have had something to do with it."

"That's right. We sort of have a prisoner code here, and that is you don't rat on anybody. I could be roughed up pretty bad if my cooperating with you gets around."

"Whatever you tell me stays with me, and perhaps my team, but I'll do whatever I can to protect you."

"Your word is good with me."

Lou nodded. "So, you think Denny Daly might be our man?"

"I told Mr. Kelly, Denny and Zippy were close, almost like brothers. When you're stuck in prison, you talk about your life, your mistakes, what you did and didn't do, and of course, the people who were there for you, and especially those who put you in this mess. Zippy believed Judge Breckinridge was responsible for his being in prison. A day didn't go by when the two of them didn't talk about it. More than once I heard Denny tell Zip that he would even Zip's score. And once you commit to something in this place, you better follow through because if you don't, it'll come back to haunt you. It means you're spineless — your word can't be trusted. Believe me, if you say you'll do something on the outside, you do it because not acting brings shame to your name. And in this place, your name is about all you've got."

"Your reputation is not good," Lou said to Henry. "You've been labeled arrogant, cocky, and a liar."

"Of course."

"Of course?"

"We're talking about survival. I've seen all kinds of personalities in this place. The wimps are destroyed. Gangs form. This is a

'survival of the fittest' place. Darwin didn't have to go to South America to discover that. All he needed to do was spend a few weeks in a penitentiary."

"I understand."

"You don't have to believe me," Henry continued. "I've read a couple of your books from the prison library, and if you're in real life like you are in your novels, then I want to help you get justice. That's why I contacted Mr. Kelly. If you want to believe I'm a liar, that's your choice. I can't do anything about that."

"I appreciate your talking with me, Henry," Lou said. "You've given me a candid view of what happens behind these walls."

"Here is another message for people on the outside," Henry began. "This is no way to rehabilitate anyone or to punish him, for that matter. It's been a slow evolutionary process, dating back to dungeons, and they haven't made much progress. People have little patience for guys who hurt or take advantage of others, and most of us understand that. But the present system has a long way to go toward helping society deal with misfits. And that's what we are — misfits."

"How much longer do you have to go?" Lou asked.

"As of this morning, I've got thirteen hundred and twenty days left until my first parole hearing."

"When you get out, look me up," Lou suggested.

"I'll do it. You may find a little competition, Mr. Searing. In my spare time — and I have a lot more than you do — I'm writing a series of mysteries."

"Good for you. A good story teller has no competitors, only fellow writers. There are millions of readers, more readers than stories to tell, and books to sell. I'll welcome your series and maybe we can do some book-signings together."

"I would enjoy that, Mr. Searing."

"'Lou' to you, okay?"

"Thanks, Lou."

After meeting to identify their goals, the 4-H students contacted the Dean of Engineering at Michigan State University and asked for an opportunity to explain their project. They explained to the dean they would need to work with a physics professor and a structural engineer.

The oval table in the dean's conference room was set for a meeting of six people with carafes of coffee and bottles of water in the center. The Dean, Dr. Edith Edwards, had invited two members of her staff to be present. Mrs. Myers and two student leaders represented the 4-H club.

Dean Edwards began. "Thank you for coming, and thank you for including Michigan State in your work."

"Thank *you*, Dean Edwards, for helping us assist detective Lou Searing in solving the murder of Judge Breckinridge," Mrs. Myers replied. "With me today are 4-H club members Becky Smith and Tom Willard who represent ten others all looking forward to the results of this meeting."

"It is nice to meet you, Becky and Tom," Dean Edwards replied. "I hope you two will consider Michigan State for your college experience, undergraduate or graduate." Becky and Tom smiled and nodded.

Dean Edwards gestured to one of two men in lab coats. "To my right is Professor Peek of the Physics Department, and to my left is Dr. Lawrence of our Engineering staff. Now, we'll listen as you explain how you think we can help you."

Tom began. "Simply stated, we need help in finding the weight that needs to be applied to a carnival-ride restraining bar before it gives way. More specifically, we need to learn whether that force varies if a person in the capsule is live or dead weight."

"Well-stated, Tom," Professor Peek replied. "Could you explain the background for your request?"

"I would, but Becky has a better understanding of it than I do."

Becky stood, holding a page of notes. "A recent court case involved a carnival ride operator and the owner of the company providing rides at a fair. A woman was flung from the Egg-Beater, supposedly causing her death. The prosecutor claimed the woman was killed falling out of the ride as it was moving and that she died because the restraining bar either gave way or was not secure when the ride began.

"The defense attorney's position was that the woman had died before the ride began to move, so she was not killed in the fall. Her toxicology report showed sufficient drugs in her system to kill her without outside action. In fact, an expert called by the defense questioned how the woman had managed to purchase a ticket and climb into the ride capsule on her own. However, the jury found the ride operator guilty of negligent homicide.

"As part of Mr. Searing's investigation of Judge Breckinridge's murder he has asked that we do an experiment to see if the woman's dead weight would exceed the holding capacity of the restraining bar. If dead weight could cause the restraining bar to fail, it would lend credence to the theory the woman was dead before her fall. A live person might be able to control that weight and not fall into the bar, causing it to give way.

Becky looked up from her notes. "It's rather complicated. Shall I try to explain further?"

"You've done an excellent job," Dr. Lawrence said with a smile. "I know exactly what Mr. Searing is looking for, and I think we can help. We may need the help of an auto manufacturer that does crash testing. They would have the technology to approximate conditions at the fair."

"That would be great," Tom replied, with Becky nodding.

The meeting ended on the hope that arrangements could be made to work with an auto company.

In his notes, Lou discovered that two people had not yet been contacted: Colon Manley and MeLissa Evans. Lou called Maggie, briefed her on the matter related to MeLissa, and suggested that

Maggie and Heather interview her. He decided to talk to Colon himself.

Lou invited Colon for a soft drink and a chat at a park in Lansing. Colon was relatively short and about thirty years old. Muscles bulged against the fabric of his knit shirt which sported the logo of the Lansing Country Club.

"Thank you for meeting with me, Colon. As I said on the phone, I'm investigating the Breckinridge murder."

"Pretty violent way to leave the earth," Colon said, shaking his head.

"Yes, it was. I understand you refused to go along with an alleged hole-in-one hit by Judge Breckinridge."

"Yes, most unfortunate. I know the rule on this because a similar thing happened to a friend of mine, who is a golf pro. In telling me his story, he made it very clear that if the ball doesn't rest in the bottom of the cup, the shot is not an ace."

"And golf is a game of rules," Lou replied.

"Exactly, and the judge should respect that, but he didn't. He had a flask of hard liquor in his golf bag, and he frequently drank from it. Anyway, he hit this shot, and the ball landed on the wet edge of the cup. Since the judge couldn't move the ball to place it anywhere for a second shot, he figured it was a hole-in-one. Two others in the group basically said, 'Looks like an ace to me.' But when I said, 'No, it's not an ace,' the fireworks began.

"I told the judge and the others that I could not attest that the ball went into the cup because it didn't. Evidently, the ace was very important to him. He said that his great-grandfather, grandfather, and father had all made holes-in-one, and he had hoped it would happen to him in his lifetime. It meant a lot to carry on this family tradition. As I said, he'd had quite a bit to drink. He just lost it, made a few threats like, 'You attest this ace, Colon, or I'll bury you!'

Then he said something like, 'If you don't say this is an ace, I'll kill you, and I mean it.'"

"I can see someone being a bit perturbed by your decision, but I can't imagine making threats," Lou said, as he wrote Win's exact words onto his notepad.

"Yeah, the others tried to calm him down. He was drunk, Mr. Searing. I didn't think I was in danger."

"I sure would have felt threatened," Lou replied. "How could you not?"

"Because it'd happened a couple of times before."

"What had happened before?"

"A couple of friends and I were with him at a bass fishing contest. He wanted us to take a huge pre-caught bass out in the boat and then he could claim to have reeled it in. When I wouldn't go along with this, he pulled the same stunt. A day or two later, it was as if he had forgotten the whole thing. We were buddies again."

"And there was a third occasion?" Lou asked.

"That was much more a matter of ethics than the ace or the bass. Now that he's dead, I guess I can talk about it. I was sitting in a bar with the judge and two of his lawyer friends. I don't know all the details, but he was telling the lawyers he was going to throw a case out because of a favor done for him by the defense attorney. The lawyers were incensed that he would even consider this. Once again, I became a thorn under his saddle."

"How so?" Lou asked.

"I interrupted and informed him that if the case were dismissed, I would report what I had overheard to the Judicial Commission. So, as he did on the golf course, he went crazy with his threats. I just held my ground."

"Was the case dismissed?"

"Yes."

"And you told the officials what you had heard?" Lou asked.

"Yes."

"Weren't you concerned for your life?"

"Actually, I had to do something. About a month earlier, a neighbor had called several times in the course of a week. She said she thought someone was stalking me from a vacant lot behind my house. It had to be the judge, or someone the judge had hired. I felt trapped, and I was scared. I prepared to evacuate with a few belongings if my house was set on fire.

"I glanced out the window on this particular night and saw movement out back. I had an idea. I went into my garage and broke down a cardboard box. Hastily, I drew a human form on the cardboard, cut it out, and attached it to a yardstick. That afternoon, in case someone came snooping around, I had set up a video camera in my downstairs bathroom window so that any movement in back of my home would be captured on film.

"That night, I went upstairs and turned on the light in my bedroom. While lying on the floor on my back, I moved the cardboard figure in front of the window, as if a person were looking out.

"Are you going to tell me this cardboard person was 'murdered'?" Lou asked.

"Exactly! A shot came through the window, shattering it and hitting the cardboard cutout. The bullet wound up in the wall over my bed. I lowered the cutout as if the person had been struck. Then I heard a car leave.

"So, who was the shooter?"

"I believe it was Win Breckinridge."

"You *believe*, or you *know*?" Lou asked.

"I didn't see his face, but I'm certain it was the judge."

"Then what happened?" Lou asked.

"Nothing, beyond my having the window repaired and the wall re-plastered."

"Did you contact the police?" Lou asked, astonished.

"No. I didn't need to; I had it all on video tape."

"Did you ever confront the judge?"

"No."

"Did the judge pass out when he next saw you?"

"No. He said, 'How's my friend Colon doing today?' Or something like that."

"Really?"

"Oh yeah, he would have denied the whole thing. 'Preposterous!' he'd have claimed."

"But if you have him on video tape…" Lou replied.

"Yes. And I have the bullet, the cardboard cutout, photos of the broken window, and the bullet hole in the wall."

"Did the judge know you had this incriminating evidence?" Lou asked.

"No. At the right time I was going to have my attorney bring it forward."

"So, the threats he made to you were about to be exposed at the time he was killed."

"Yes, and not only the threats, but the names of those who had witnessed the threats."

"You had the goods on him." Lou concluded.

"You *bet* I did!"

"But, now after all of this, the judge is murdered."

"Yes, and I killed him to make sure he paid the full price. If I hadn't, he could have threatened others into disputing my evidence, and once again justice would not have been served."

"*You* killed him?" Lou repeated, dumbfounded.

"Of *course* not! But, I figured that was what you were thinking. I mean, how would you like to live every moment of your life wondering if a rifle is trained on you? Or, once I made my complaint known, who knows how many ways I might have died before the trial? So, once you know about this, it's obvious I should want to put this all to rest by getting rid of the man."

"I agree," Lou said. "You *are* convincing."

"There's only one thing wrong with thinking I would have killed him."

"What's that?" Lou asked.

"My IQ — intelligence quotient," Conlon replied. "I'd hope people think that, if I were going to kill him, I would be more resourceful. Killing him at a fair with thousands of people around, with the sheriff and a crew of deputies on duty in a command center a few feet away? Poison is much easier. Or, inviting him to go hunting and making *him* the prey. Either someone without a lot of brain power or someone acting on impulse would kill him at a county fair."

"I see," Lou replied. "Does anyone else know what you've just told me?"

"Yes. The judge's wife."

"*She* killed her husband?" Lou asked.

"One significant factor precludes that also, Mr. Searing."

"IQ?" Lou reasoned.

"Exactly. She wouldn't give up her life to knock off the scumbag. Smart people murder with their minds, Mr. Searing. We don't do it by conventional means."

"Is there any threat to you, or Mrs. Breckinridge for that matter, now that the judge is dead?"

"None. We're free, and it's a relief, a tremendous relief."

"Why should Mrs. Breckinridge need her husband dead?"

"*She'll* have to answer that. I know why, but you need to hear it from Bonnie. I've told you all I know, but I don't discuss other people's relationships."

"That's fair. Thanks for talking with me, Colon."

"Normally I would say, 'I hope you find the murderer,' but in this case, I hope he, she, or they are never discovered. Win's death brought some of us peace of mind. We have our lives back. What a marvelous feeling!"

"Sorry, but I'm pretty sure we'll solve this one, Colon. It's only a matter of time."

Maggie and Heather made arrangements to meet attorney MeLissa Evans in her downtown Lansing office. MeLissa, blonde and blue-eyed, used her looks to effectively manipulate judges, witnesses, and juries. MeLissa was in her early to mid-thirties; not only was she beautiful, but she was smart, and a fine attorney.

Maggie and Heather steered their motorized chairs into attorney Evans' office in front of a large walnut desk. Framed degrees from prestigious colleges and universities hung on the walls. A bouquet of flowers graced a credenza. A brass name plate on her desk reminded anyone sitting across from her that this was the office of M-E-L-I-S-S-A E-V-A-N-S.

Maggie spoke first. "Whenever I think of someone who shares your name, I think it is spelled, MaLissa."

"Well, my Dad's name was Mel, and my mother's name was Lisa. Does that explain it?" MeLissa continued. "It is nice to meet you," extending her hand in greeting to each woman. "I've enjoyed Lou's books, so I know the parts you two have played in his investigations."

"Mr. Searing is a pleasure to work with," Maggie replied and Heather nodded.

"I can imagine. He seems genuine, and with your help, he solves the crimes."

"Our track record has been pretty good," Maggie agreed.

"Is Mr. Kelly as computer-savvy as he's portrayed in the books?" MeLissa asked.

"He has a sharp mind, and he has a way of finding facts. He is a mature personality so he keeps Lou from doing anything he might regret later."

"The four of you seem a compatible meeting of minds. So, you wanted to talk to me?" MeLissa asked, her smile fading.

"Yes. Your name has come up in our inquiries, and we need to clarify our information."

"Well, if I've been portrayed in less than honorable fashion, I certainly want to set the record straight. What have you heard of me?" MeLissa asked.

Maggie began, "You realize that what you tell us will be shared with Mr. Searing and Jack, but *not* with anyone else."

"Thank you. I appreciate that."

Maggie continued. "We understand you've tried some cases in Judge Breckinridge's court."

"That's true. Several, actually."

"We've also heard about after-hours meetings in the judge's chambers."

"I was afraid you'd mention that. I'd like to explain."

Before MeLissa responded, she took some papers from her desk drawer and set them before her.

"The judge and I have had many issues over the years. Working with him was a challenge for both of us."

"What do you mean by a challenge?" Maggie asked.

"We saw the law differently. I would say he looked down on women. He was odd — that's the best way to answer your question. Since I'm a suspect in the judge's death, I want to clear the air.

I won't deny being in the judge's chambers often, and after hours. That doesn't look appropriate, and I suppose it isn't. However, why I was there and what was going on is absolutely no one's business. But people talk, so I will explain."

Heather and Maggie were now poised with pens above paper.

"One of my weaknesses as a trial attorney is cross-examination. Judge Breckinridge was experienced and very intelligent. I thought that I might pay him for coaching. He was very busy, and he said that the only time he could help me was after hours."

"Your husband was supportive of you and the judge working together in the evening, in his office?"

"Definitely. It was helping, too. I was learning effective techniques."

Maggie decided to cut to the chase. "Did you kill Judge Breckinridge?"

"Did I…?" MeLissa gaped in shock at Maggie's question.

"Did you kill Judge Breckinridge?" Maggie repeated her question.

"Why would you ask such a bizarre question?"

"Any number of reasons. Perhaps he owed you a lot of money and wasn't going to pay you back," Heather reasoned. "Perhaps you owed him money and had no plans to pay him. The judge being dead erases the debt."

"I see your reasoning, but I had only respect and admiration for Judge Breckinridge."

"I trust you know that people outside the judge's office had other impressions."

"We knew that, but we decided to let them talk. We could only do what we thought was best."

"Thank you for meeting with us," Maggie said, reaching into her attaché. "Here is my card if you wish to talk with me further about this matter."

MeLissa nodded, now looking pale and shaken.

The two detectives skillfully wheeled out of the attorney's office into the lobby area, thanked the receptionist for her help, and left.

The next morning, an article bearing the lead, **"Breckinridge and Evans Shared Chambers After Hours,"** appeared in the *Lansing State Journal*. The article stated:

> *As the investigation into the murder of Judge Winston Breckinridge continues, an anonymous source reports that the judge, murdered at the Ingham County Fair on August 8, and attorney MeLissa Evans spent many evening hours in the judge's chambers. Police do not know whether this relates to the judge's murder, but detectives speculate concerning a possible tie to the judge's death. The investigation continues.*

This news caught MeLissa Evans off-guard. Devastated and angry, she became convinced that Maggie and Heather had gone directly to the news media with her revelations.

She dialed Maggie's number from the business card. When Maggie answered, MeLissa shouted, "How dare you?! You told me you would not pass along what I shared with you, but, there it is in the paper!"

"I don't know what you are talking about," Maggie replied, trying to imagine the by-line and text of the article.

"The *Lansing State Journal* published an article saying that I spent numerous night-time hours in the judge's chambers."

"The writer could not have quoted me because neither I nor Heather have talked to a reporter. In fact, as we promised you, our information is confidential."

"You two are the only ones I have spoken to. Who else would have called in the information?" MeLissa exclaimed. "Every media outlet in the state has been calling to verify the newspaper item. How could you do this to me?"

"Listen, Mrs. Evans. I can't control what you believe, but we did not call the newspaper. In fact, we did not call anyone. Do you understand?" Maggie pleaded. "I don't know the newspaper's source, but I'm sure many people knew of your situation."

"But *nobody* knows!"

"How about others who work in the court?" Maggie responded. "Someone the judge may have told? How about the janitor who perhaps saw the two of you together? It seems your 'secret' coaching involved more people than the two of you expected."

"Those are possibilities, but I believe you are responsible for telling the reporter!" MeLissa said, still quite angry.

"I regret that, because it's *not* true," Maggie once again protested.

"You've not heard the last from me, Mrs. McMillan. This is slander become libel, and I will have my name cleared! I'll sue you for all you have for these scandalous inferences." The conversation ended civilly, but MeLissa remained agitated and angry.

Maggie informed Lou regarding the meeting with MeLissa and the newspaper article. Immediately, Lou called Sheriff Lloyd.

"I appreciate freedom of the press, Sheriff, but this morning's article compromises my investigation into the judge's murder,"

Lou began. "Maggie obtained information yesterday and had promised Mrs. Evans that what she said would remain confidential. Then within twelve hours the whole reading public and all media outlets that took it from the wires know of her regular visits with the judge."

"I'm sorry about this, Lou. One of my detectives got an anonymous call. That person said the two shared after-hours visits in his chambers on many occasions. Apparently this person called the newspaper. None of my staff contacted the newspaper, and the editor did not check with me before running the story."

"That editor missed a lecture in college — about a cardinal rule of journalism. No competent editor would print that article without checking with you first."

"He's new, comes from a small-town paper in Idaho. He's a nice guy, but green behind the ears."

"That's no excuse. Have you talked with him?" Lou asked.

"Yes, first thing. I've been trying to reach Mrs. Evans to explain, but I can't get through — her phone is tied up."

"Did the editor tell you his source?" Lou asked.

"No, said he wanted to protect the source."

"Well, it needs to become public soon, because Mrs. Evans believes Maggie and Heather provided the story to the paper. And quite frankly, I am concerned for the safety of these two women. After all, she may have killed the judge and I can't risk a person with that mentality possibly responding irrationally. Now she feels painted into a corner, and a caged tiger can be dangerous. I need the name of the informant as soon as possible."

"I'll get back to you as soon as I can, Lou. Wait — let me put you on hold. I have a call from the newspaper."

Just as Lou was about to hang up and take a couple of calls, the sheriff came back on. "Sorry to keep you waiting, Lou. Get this: the informant was the judge's wife, Bonnie Breckinridge."

"Her way to bring down Evans?"

"Could be."

"We need to rein in Mrs. Breckinridge," Lou suggested. "Her name keeps coming up. I've talked to her, and she claimed to have had nothing to do with the murder. But she admitted to Heather she had played a part in the crime, and we haven't figured out just what that means."

"I'll arrange for officers for Maggie and Heather, and I'll have Mrs. Evans' movements monitored for a while. Sorry this happened, but we had nothing to do with it, Lou."

"I understand. Thanks, Sheriff."

nine

After Jack was briefed concerning what Lou, Maggie and Heather had unearthed, he believed that Mrs. Breckinridge was at the heart of the case. With Lou's encouragement, Jack volunteered to learn as much as he could about her.

Within the hour, Jack had discovered that Bonnie Breckinridge's maiden name was Watkins; she had been valedictorian of her 1979 Alpena High School class; and she had majored in pre-law at Michigan State University. While in college, Bonnie discovered a strong interest in the environment, and she wanted to join the movement to conserve natural resources. She quickly realized that law and accompanying rules were the key; only changes in the law would cut emissions, clean lakes and rivers, and minimize commercial waste. With her fighting spirit, she would join others who were taking on giant corporations. These companies depended on the *status quo* to keep profits up, to keep stockholders happy, and to attract more investors.

Bonnie met Winston Breckinridge at MSU. Ironically, Winston was also a pre-law student, but his interests leaned toward the other side of the environmental question. He saw that he could earn millions defending tobacco companies and protecting corporations from government and enraged consumers, all of whom were filing what he considered "frivolous" lawsuits.

The law of nature that opposites attract was proven when Bonnie and Win debated environmental issues with friends in the student union, leading to an admiration for each other's skill and intelligence. They enjoyed cheap dates tossing bread to the ducks on the Red Cedar River, then an occasional dinner at Beggar's Banquet in East Lansing. Love grew until they arrived at the conclusion that they should get married; they would raise a little Breckinridge, one genetically prepared to be either the next Ralph Nader or the next Donald Trump.

Their wedding, a week after Win graduated from law school, was a small affair performed by a Justice of the Peace in the MSU botanical gardens. The small group of family and friends gathered for punch and cookies following the ceremony. Instead of focusing on love and harmony for the newly-married couple, consensus among the guests was that these two were not made for each other; nor was the marriage made in Heaven. Several guests had stories of a mismatch that had turned into a happy and long marriage. But despite the stories, the word "annulment" joined with the words "two weeks" to describe what they felt was a mistake were revealed too late to save the expense of a wedding.

Bonnie and Win were ready to prove wrong those who predicted their marriage was doomed. They both took jobs, making a conscious effort to save as much money as possible. Bonnie worked to save the environment, and Win worked for corporations. Bonnie was a Democrat and a conservative Catholic. Win was a Republican and a Catholic convert who seldom, if ever, attended Mass. Initially, dinner — steak for Win and salad for Bonnie — was fun. Conversation was lively, and neither lacked for an interesting story to tell.

They began to tease one another about their opposing views in a joking fashion, but over time, humorous teasing gave way to disrespect and humiliation. At social events, Win and Bonnie bragged of who had won arguments, how it could be possible for an environmentalist to live with a corporate attorney, a conservative Catholic with a

Catholic in name only, a Democrat with a Republican, a carnivore with a vegetarian. Slowly but surely, Win and Bonnie themselves began to wonder whether their marriage would last.

As part of his research, Jack interviewed Bonnie Breckinridge's sister, Joan Watkins, by phone. Near the end of their conversation, Jack hit on something that might be important when he asked, "Is Bonnie capable of killing Win?"

"You know, I can't get that out of my mind," Joan replied. "I think so."

"So, you think she could have killed him?" Jack repeated Joan's answer, encouraging her to continue voicing her thoughts.

"Well, yes, and no. No, because she has respect for life, being a conservative Catholic. I think she loved the man, just didn't love much *about* him, if that makes any sense. On the other hand, not having him around would certainly make her life much happier."

"As a Catholic, wouldn't she have a difficult time taking a life?" Jack asked.

"Yes, but she said Win would never agree to a divorce."

"Because Catholics don't approve of divorce?" Jack asked.

"It had nothing to do with religion. He told her repeatedly that a divorce would hinder his political career."

"And, she seems quite intelligent," Jack added. "Murder can result from deep emotion, but if she killed him, she had to realize that her chances of getting off were practically nil. She probably wasn't so miserable that years in a women's penitentiary would be a welcome change."

"I agree," Joan said. "But, if she saw an opportunity to frame someone, or to hire the murder done with strong assurance that she wouldn't be caught, I can see her going ahead with it." Joan took a deep breath. "Mr. Kelly, I'm not accusing my sister of murder.

I'm simply thinking about what might have been going through her mind."

"I understand," Jack said. "Did Win have any skeletons in his closet that you know of?"

"Bonnie didn't seem to keep anything back in talking with me. She was quite certain he was having an affair with an attorney by the name of Evans. Someone in the court office had told her about night visits. When she confronted Win, he said a certain staffer was getting back at him for not getting a promotion, and he would never act inappropriately."

"Did he gamble or do drugs?" Jack asked.

"She never told me about either. Now, Bonnie may have known about it, but if she did, she didn't mention it to me."

"Thank you for talking with me, Joan."

"I can't imagine Bonnie killing Win, but I've been open and candid. I trust you and Mr. Searing or I wouldn't have said a word."

"Thank you," Jack said. "We appreciate your trust."

"One more thing. I've been holding this back, but maybe it's relevant. Bonnie was expelled from the Lansing Law College in the mid-1980s."

"Really? What's the story behind that?" Jack asked.

"I don't know for sure," Joan replied. "The family never said anything, just that the expulsion devastated Bonnie. She sought professional help, but after a year or so, she seemed to move beyond it, becoming a highly-respected social activist. And she turned to painting. It was a good move for her."

Lou thought it best to work on the source of the tattoo seen on the woman's leg the night of the murder. He remembered that a friend was related to Jackie June, the owner of a tattoo parlor in California. Later that evening, he called the West Coast.

"Ms. June, this is Lou Searing. Your friend, Charlotte, suggested I call you. She thought you might be able to help me on a murder investigation."

"She e-mailed me that you might be calling, and I'm Jackie, okay? How can I help?"

"A suspect in a murder here in Michigan has a tattoo at the base of her right leg. The tattoo is of the scales of justice, except the scales are uneven; one pan is significantly higher than the other. I wondered whether you've a trade book with pictures of various tattoos that you show to clients."

"There's not *one*, Lou — there are several. Our industry has a few books that most of us use, but there are several more out there."

"That's not what I wanted to hear, Jackie."

"Sorry. There are also Internet resources. That's probably a better bet."

"How do I find what I need?" Lou asked.

"Go onto the Internet and put 'tattoo designs' into the search window. You'll likely find all you want or need. Most sites have a search feature. If I were you, I'd search for 'scales of justice' and see what comes up."

"Okay, thanks."

"My guess is you won't find one with the scales tilted. That sounds like it would need to be designed in a parlor."

"Thank you so much," Lou replied. "One more question, please."

"Sure."

"I'll ask it in the form of a statement," Lou replied. "I assume there's no way to know where someone gets a tattoo, short of asking them."

"That's right. There are no initials, no signatures, no copyright, and no one web site. The only way to really know is to ask the person wearing it."

"Thanks, Jackie."

"I just thought of something. There's another possible source of information — chat rooms for people with tattoos. You could go into several and ask if anyone knows of a tattoo with tilted scales of justice."

"Okay. Thanks, Jackie. You've been a lot of help."

"Call back if you have more questions, Lou."

As Lou reviewed the case, reading and rereading his notebook of interview material, he realized he was feeling overwhelmed. He thought, *If I'm on overload, others must be too.* Lou proposed to Carol that they host a beach party with time for review of what they knew and what they still needed to discover. Carol happily agreed.

Lou and Carol distributed verbal and e-mail invitations for the next afternoon. Jack was encouraged to bring Elaine. Maggie was to bring her husband and daughter, if he could be torn from his almost-daily eighteen holes of golf. Heather was invited to bring Wendy, her roommate at Western Michigan University.

Twenty-four hours later, the four gathered in Lou and Carol's living room with notes to discuss their case. The view of Lake Michigan competed with business for their attention, but even with distractions of people, boats, freighters, and unique cloud formations, the investigative team devoted 90 per cent of their energy to the case, which they now called Murder at the Ingham County Fair."

Lou had brought out an easel holding large sheets of paper that could be marked up, torn off, and stuck to wall-space in the living and dining rooms. While Jack, Maggie, Heather, and Lou organized notes and thoughts, Carol, Elaine, Tom, and Wendy began preparations for a picnic following the work session.

Lou began. "Thanks for coming today. I suggested that we meet because, in spite of my age, if I need a summary of what we've learned, you three might be in the same boat. We'll work for as long as it takes, and then there'll be food and relaxation."

"Good idea," Heather said. "I have a list of our suspects and a summary of their information. And the program I designed can analyze the data, in a sense, and determine the likelihood that each suspect is the murderer."

"That's great," Lou replied. "Heather and her computer program have done much of the work for us. OK, let's start solving this crime." Each of the four had a laptop in front of him or her. Heather copied and sent the computer analysis to each machine so they were all informed.

"On the left side of your screen is a list of the suspects," Heather explained. "They are not alphabetical, but are ranked from the most likely to have committed the crime to the least likely. On the right side is supporting information you provided on each suspect."

"This is fabulous, Heather! You've done what I was about to suggest we do. I'm delighted," Lou said. "You've cut the time in half and we all have the same information."

"It's simply what you asked me to do."

"Great! Now we only need to review these files, rather than create them on paper and stick them to the walls."

"Technology has officially entered the Lou Searing world of crime investigation!" Jack proclaimed. Lou, Maggie, and Jack also understood what a valuable addition to the team Heather had proven to be.

Flipping hamburgers on the grill, Tom McMillan said to Elaine and Carol, "I'm glad they're happy, or as happy as is possible when they're discussing murder."

"Amen," Elaine said. "They're so talented as individuals, their collective minds must be awesome. No wonder they're so effective."

"And, they respect one another," Carol added. "It's a good team, and I know Lou is very pleased and thankful to have Jack, Maggie, and Heather working on his cases."

While Carol and Wendy cut up a variety of fresh summer vegetables for salad, the investigative team shared perceptions of the information Heather had provided.

"Do we all agree that Bonnie Breckinridge is the lead suspect?" Lou asked.

"I think she has to be high on the list, but I don't think she pulled the trigger," Jack agreed. "She admitted to Heather that she was party to the killing, so taking her at her word, she is at least an accomplice, and possibly the murderer."

"I agree," Maggie added.

"Could I add my two cents worth?" Heather asked, carefully listening to the others.

"Please do. That's why we're together — to hear each other's thoughts," Lou replied.

Heather took a deep breath before she spoke. "When Mrs. Breckinridge told me she was a party to the murder, she said she had told Mr. Searing she had nothing to do with it. When I asked her why she admitted this to me, she said, 'Because you're a woman.' That stuck with me, and I'm not sure I understand it. If I had experienced a difficult marriage, I might understand her motivation. But she knew I would tell Lou, which would implicate her. So, do you three have any idea what she might have meant in telling *me* she had a part in the murder?"

Maggie replied first, "I think she told you the truth — that she had aided in the murder. But I also think that she wanted us to know she hadn't killed the judge."

Jack added, "I agree. By telling you, she's helping us solve it. But when her part is divulged, she may be in a better position with the prosecutor's office by having assisted in bringing her husband's murderer to justice."

"If you're right, why didn't she just say who did it?" Lou asked.

"If she did, she would be a traitor to whoever killed him, and that would be too much to divulge," Heather reasoned.

"Good point," Lou admitted. "Okay, enough about Mrs. B. How about another possibility?" Lou asked, while checking the suspect list.

"I'd like to bring up Denny, the guy recently released from prison who befriended Zippy Roelof," Jack suggested. "I think we can drop him from our list because he has a good grip on life at the moment and a good-paying job. I can't imagine him throwing all that over to avenge a friend still in prison."

"But, we don't know the unwritten rules of the prison," Lou replied. "Normally I would agree, but these guys make promises, and maybe not following through would lead to trouble down the road."

Maggie added, "Remember, we need to realize that whoever pulled the trigger did so with some assistance from Mrs. B., so we also need to establish a connection."

"Good point," Heather replied. "Denny could have played a part like Mrs. B.; he can report a dead judge to Roelof, but needn't pull the trigger himself."

"Okay, we'll move Denny down on the list," Lou decided. "Now, what about the lady with the unbalanced scales tattoo?"

"My guess is, she's gotten out of Dodge," Jack said.

"Our best way to identify her is to find out who gave her the tattoo," Heather offered.

"I think it's likely she got the tattoo in the Lansing area," Jack added.

"I wonder if the media would help." Maggie said. "WLNS has a CrimeStoppers segment, during which they show photos of people with aliases or anything else helpful in identifying them. We could request they broadcast a drawing of the unbalanced scale of justice, asking anyone who has seen the tattoo to call the police."

"Great idea," Lou said energetically. "Jack, please run it by Sheriff Lloyd. If he approves, contact WLNS — News 6 and see if their CrimeStoppers segment can assist us."

"Will do."

"I think people who get tattoos tend to show them to family and friends," Lou mused. "It's something they paid for, and I think they would want to show it off."

"You're right," Heather agreed. "On campus, tattoos are always a topic of conversation. Students talk about those seen in the dorm, or people show off one just acquired."

"There's one caution to consider," Maggie added. "The tattoo could have been temporary. You can get one for three to five dollars at various events. Someone may call in a tattoo, but when we get to the person named, the mark could be gone. We'd have a difficult time proving a given person ever sported a tattoo."

"Thanks for that downer, Maggie, however realistic," Lou said with a smile. "Any other suspects to discuss?"

"I wonder about Les Grant, the Democratic candidate," Maggie said. "Everyone says he can't be a killer, and yet, that might be reason to consider him a serious suspect. Sometimes the innocent-acting grandmother turns out to be an axe-murderer."

"Okay. I don't think anyone disagrees," Lou said. "I'd like to add Colon, the golf partner who videotaped someone he thinks was Judge Breckinridge shooting into his home."

"I agree," Jack replied. "If Colon had been in front of that window instead of a cardboard cutout, we might be looking into *his* murder instead of the judge's."

"Does everyone agree that Randy Pollard, the prisoner working the fairgrounds — the one who discovered the body — is not a suspect?" Heather asked.

"I want to keep him low on the list — I don't think he is involved," Lou responded. "Anyone else?"

"MeLissa Evans has to be considered," Jack said.

"Yes. She's someone who might realistically work with Mrs. Breckinridge. She fits the comment to Heather that 'a woman would understand.'"

"She had no strong reason to kill the judge unless there was some blackmail going on that we haven't discovered," Lou summarized. "I think we've covered the most logical suspects to date. We need to do a few more interviews and then dig, question, probe, and figure it all out."

Heather spoke up. "Nobody's mentioned Norah Hartmann, the wife of the man Bill Thompson killed."

Maggie replied, "What hit me hard was her comment: 'If I wanted revenge, I would have killed Thompson, not the judge!' That made sense to me, and I dismissed her as a serious suspect."

Jack continued the listing. "Another possibility we didn't mention is Zippy Roelof, the carnival worker who was convicted of negligent homicide. His attorney was trying to prove the woman in the Egg-Beater was dead before the 'malfunction' threw her out of the ride."

"Again, I don't see Zippy as a murderer," Lou said. "I think we can safely put him aside."

"Are we finished?" Lou asked.

"Time for dinner," Carol called from the deck. She had a sixth sense about when Lou's meetings were about to wrap up. "Everyone is on their own. Hamburgers and hotdogs are on the grill, chips, fruit, and baked beans are in the kitchen, and drinks are on the counter. You can go out onto the beach, sit on the deck, or stay inside."

The eight friends held hands as Lou said Grace. Even Samm lay on the floor with her paws together in front of her. Following the prayer, Lou looked toward Heather and said, "And before we begin, belated birthday congratulations are in order for Heather, who recently turned twenty-one!"

Carol began rhythmic clapping as Maggie began the birthday song. All seven voices could be heard. Heather was a bit taken aback, but she smiled and thanked everyone.

"How did you know it was my birthday, Mr. Searing?" she asked, blushing.

"Well, a good detective does more than analyze clues."

"It probably means paying attention to Maggie!" Heather laughed, while Maggie nodded.

As they enjoyed dinner on the deck, relishing a breeze off the lake, Lou's cell phone rang.

"Excuse me," Lou said, moving into the kitchen. "Let's hope this is someone from church, or something equally routine."

But the phone relayed a now-familiar voice. "Lou, this is Gene Lloyd. There's been a strange development in the case, and I want you to know about it before you read it in the paper."

"I appreciate that, Sheriff. I don't like surprises."

"Bonnie Breckinridge was found dead in her East Lansing home about fifteen minutes ago."

"Hmm, that's unexpected," Lou said, his mind going in several directions, trying to understand who and how.

"She was shot short-range, like the judge, probably with a silenced pistol or revolver. Her friend Nicki Nelson found her and called 911. My deputies are talking to neighbors now. You and Jack might want to visit the scene."

"We'll head out right now," Lou replied. "Thanks for the call."

Lou closed his phone, put it in his pocket and returned to the group enjoying strawberry shortcake on the back porch.

"Well, here is news for the team. Bonnie Breckinridge has been murdered. Jack, I'll need you to come with me to East Lansing. I'll call Tom Howard who has a single engine plane. If he's available and willing, we could be in Lansing in about forty-five minutes. Maggie and Heather, if you want to stay overnight, we've got room and would love to have you. I'll call with any new information. We might be working on this into the night."

Tom was available and, as always, willing to fly his plane. Lou and Jack would meet him at Grand Haven Municipal Airport.

Jack took a couple of big bites of dessert, washed them down with a gulp of coffee, and followed Lou out to his car. On the way to the airport, the two men traded ideas.

"Might be suicide, Lou," Jack said, citing an obvious possibility.

"Could be, but I doubt it," Lou replied. "I think she was killed for saying too much."

"You think admitting she was complicit in the murder may have been too much to offer the authorities?" Jack asked.

"I'm not sure at the moment. Obviously, someone viewed her as a threat."

When Lou and Jack arrived at the airport, Lou thanked Tom profusely for providing the flight to Lansing. "You're welcome, Lou. Any time I can help, I will. You know that."

"It's much appreciated, Tom. Is the weather okay that way?"

"I filed a flight plan and checked the weather, and it should be a smooth flight to Lansing. But, we might encounter some rough weather coming back, depending on how long you plan to stay."

Lou called the sheriff's office to ask someone to meet them at Capitol City Airport's General Aviation Terminal and take them to the scene of the crime. Almost an hour later, Tom touched down in Lansing. As the single-engine Cessna taxied to the terminal, Lou could see an Ingham County Sheriff's vehicle waiting to take them to Harrison Road in East Lansing.

When they arrived at the Breckinridge home, an officer waved them past the yellow crime-scene tape and into the house. They went immediately to the bedroom where the medical examiner was certifying death. Bonnie's body lay on the floor between the king-size bed and the door.

"Look at this, Lou," Jack said, pointing to Bonnie's leg. Lou glanced down at the faded tattoo, an uneven scales of justice.

"That's odd. Maybe she was the woman at the Republican booth the night of Win's murder," Lou said.

"Or, if she wasn't at the fair, someone else has the same tattoo," Jack reasoned.

Lou was relieved the crime scene investigators had located a bullet, for a ballistic analysis could indicate whether the same weapon had been used for both murders. There was no suicide note in Bonnie's home, nor was there obvious evidence of who might have committed this crime. Detectives continued to interview neighbors, but no one reported seeing anything unusual — no strangers, no unrecognized vehicles in the area. The neighborhood was astir, of course, given the event, but, as after the judge's death, there was a noticeable lack of shock among the Breckinridge neighbors.

Lou and Jack re-interviewed several neighbors, but most could contribute nothing. Then an elderly neighbor, Mrs. Norman, mentioned something that may have made the trip from Grand Haven worthwhile.

"I saw a woman walking up and down the street, acting a bit nervous," Mrs. Norman said. "You know, like she was waiting for someone to pick her up and was perturbed because the ride was late. I didn't recognize the woman, so she wasn't a neighbor. I keep pretty close tabs on my neighbors, you see. Call me a busy-body, but I think a human neighborhood watchdog is a pretty good idea."

"Do you recall anything about the woman?" Lou asked. "A hair-style, purse, clothing?"

"Well, she was slender. I think she had a purse, but I can't be sure. She wasn't college-aged, and she wasn't old."

"That gives us quite a range," Jack offered.

"Sorry. If I'd known about Bonnie, I'd have taken a photo with my digital camera. I just noticed a woman I didn't recognize walking up and down the block."

"Was she Caucasian?" Lou asked.

"Yes, medium height, medium age, medium weight — guess I'm no help at all."

"You're very helpful, and we appreciate your information," Jack offered.

Suddenly Mrs. Norman brightened. "Wait! I do recall something; she had a dog. That's it! She had a dog, and I remember it now because the dog did its business on Luther Johnson's lawn, and she didn't pick up after it. Luther will go berserk when he finds *that* gift!"

"Good memory. What breed of dog?" Jack asked.

"Hmmm, you've got me there."

"What color was the dog? How big or small?" Lou asked.

"It wasn't black or white, but other than that, I don't recall. It was just a medium dog. It wasn't little, and it wasn't big."

"Do you recall anything else?" Jack asked.

"No. I guess she was an ordinary woman with an ordinary dog. I can't imagine this is helpful, but it's what I remember."

"Ordinary is good, because it rules out the extra-ordinary," Lou explained. "So, thank you Mrs. Norman, you've given us a lot of helpful information."

Lou and Jack informed Sheriff Lloyd and his deputies of what they'd learned, coordinating activities and taking a few minutes to consider possible suspects and motives. When they returned to the airport about ten o'clock, the moon or stars weren't visible, but neither was any lightning.

Tom Howard had stayed at the airport with a good book. Between chapters he had checked the weather, and he had become concerned.

"Are we going to Grand Haven tonight?" Lou asked.

"We'll give it a shot," Tom replied. "There's a strong front crossing Lake Michigan, but we'll monitor it from the air. Hope you guys brought toothbrushes because there's a good chance I'll put it down before we get to Grand Haven. I don't take chances."

"Good. We don't need a pilot who takes chances," Lou said, thankful for Tom's common sense.

The plane gained altitude as Tom took his plane due west. He listened to comments from other pilots in the airspace and also tuned into the weather frequency on his radio. Finally he had heard too many warnings to risk flying farther.

"Lou, I'm taking her down. This front is heavy and I can't get to Grand Haven ahead of it nor can I go high enough to get over it. So we're going to put down in Ionia."

"You're the boss, my friend," Lou replied calmly.

As Tom landed the plane at the airport, considerable lightning flashed off to the west and the wind was picking up. Tom taxied to the airport office and wasted no time in tying down the craft. As the men entered the terminal office, the winds really began to blow and rain came down in sheets.

"You managed that without a moment to spare," Jack said, praising Tom.

"Yes. In retrospect it might have been better never to have left Lansing but based on the information I had, I decided to fly."

"What do we do now?" Jack asked.

"I'll call Phil at the Motel 6, and someone will come and get us. This rough a system will take several hours to blow through.

I wouldn't recommend that Carol or Elaine try to come and get you, either."

"No problem," Lou responded. "You mentioned Phil — you're on a first-name basis with someone at a motel in Ionia?" Lou asked.

"When you fly as often as I do, you make contacts at most cities and airports. Phil will have rooms for us, and he'll bring us back in the morning."

Lou called home to learn that because of the approaching storm, Maggie and family, as well as Heather, Wendy and Elaine had headed for home.

"Tom has us safely in Ionia," Lou assured Carol. "The storms coming off the lake were too strong to tackle."

"Good thinking. Thank him for me, will you?" Carol asked, relieved to have Lou and Jack safely on *terra firma*. "I'll see you tomorrow, Lou. Love you."

"Love you, too," Lou replied.

Lou called Maggie, as he knew she would be curious. She answered and got right to the point. "Did you two solve the murder?"

"Nope, 'fraid not," Lou replied. "We just have more to add to the files. One more murder, one less suspect. A couple of things might be helpful: Bonnie Breckinridge had a scales of justice tattoo on her right lower calf, and a neighbor saw a nervous-looking woman with a dog walking in the neighborhood before the murder."

"Really?" asked Maggie, surprised with the tattoo remark. "So, was Bonnie the woman at the booth the night of the judge's murder?"

"That's what I surmised, but I decided that without thinking. Jack pointed out that someone else might have a similar tattoo, and the judge's wife may not have been the woman at the fair."

"I understand, but there's something significant about her tattoo," Maggie said.

"We need to find something to tell us where she got it. Then, assuming it's the same artist, we'll know where the other woman got her tattoo and maybe we can identify her."

"A search warrant's routine following a murder, so I'll ask for access to the Breckinridge's financial records, checkbooks, credit card statements, and any computers."

"Good. Thanks."

"Well, it might be fair to say that someone killed Bonnie because she knew too much, blabbed too much, or is viewed as a traitor," Lou summarized. "Either we have two separate cases, or our one case has become a lot more complicated."

"Or, has become clearer," Maggie added. "Now we ask, 'Who wanted the judge dead, and his wife dead as well?'"

"We're jumping to conclusions without any facts," Lou said. "Bonnie could have killed her husband, and because she did, someone wanted her to pay for that crime. Lots of variables involved."

"I think her murderer is the person that she helped indirectly when she was 'a party' to her husband's death," Maggie said. "But there are a lot of things to consider. You're right, we need facts to substantiate theories."

ten

AUGUST 15TH • GRAND HAVEN, MICHIGAN

At nine-thirty the Cessna touched down in Grand Haven and taxied up to the airport office. Lou was extremely grateful. "Tom, you're a good friend. Thanks for giving of your time and talent. I'll pay whatever you ask."

"It's on the house, Lou."

"I don't think so," Lou replied. "If you won't take money, I'll make a donation in your name to a favorite charity."

"If you feel you must donate, give a little to LOVE, Inc. — that's In the Name of Christ. They do a lot of good," Tom said, nodding.

"Will do, and thanks again for helping us."

"The pleasure was mine," Tom replied with a smile. "And, my invitation stands if you need another ride to solve the case. I'm serious."

Arriving home, Lou found Carol in the kitchen enjoying a cookie and a cup of tea. Carol was glad to see Lou safely home. He kissed her on the forehead, poured himself some coffee, took a chocolate chip cookie, and sat down. He was tired and thankful to be home.

After getting caught up with Carol, learning about some fallen limbs in front of the house, and wondering if he lost any material on his computer during the previous night's power outage, he called Maggie.

"So, what's your brain telling you now?" Maggie asked.

"My brain is playing the 'What If' game, and I need to work through some ideas. I can't shake the notion that the judge was murdered by someone he had mistreated terribly with words or actions."

"That seems basic to me, Lou."

"In that case, the strongest suspect would be Colon, the guy the judge allegedly shot at — or thought he was shooting at — while Colon pretended to be standing in his upstairs bedroom window."

"Yes, but then, why would Colon have anything against the judge's wife?" Maggie asked.

"Unless Colon had agreed to kill the judge with Bonnie's help," Lou replied.

"And, before her murder, Bonnie was admitting to more than simply assisting the murderer and Colon needed to shut her up to save himself," Maggie hypothesized.

Lou dunked a second cookie into his coffee and let it soak a few seconds before plopping half of it into his mouth.

"But, interestingly enough, Colon's feud with the judge was non-political, not related to Win's actions or statements from the bench. Maybe that's where this case is going," Lou pondered. "Maybe we're assuming it had something to do with the election or his job, when in fact, it's related to something we would normally disregard. We always need to consider possibilities beyond the obvious."

"That's hard to do when the solution often lies within the obvious," Maggie added.

"That's true. I keep thinking that maybe the judge was murdered by Wilma Simmons, the Domestic Union president."

"If she killed both Breckinridges, maybe one client needed both of them dead."

"Lester Grant?" Lou suggested.

"He was convincing when he said all politicians know about campaign back-stabbing and play the game," Maggie answered. "Besides, what would you expect him to say, Lou?"

"Good point. Unless I have facts that convince me someone is lying, I take him or her at his or her word."

Professor Lawrence had contacted engineers at Ford Motor Company Headquarters in Dearborn to ask for their assistance with the 4-H'ers' project. Ford engineers and technicians were most willing to assist in the experiment. The company that made the Egg-Beater was also a party to the testing. A lot was riding on the results of the experiment.

In the first phase, sensors were attached to the security bar of an Egg-Beater capsule, which was mounted on a standard circular rail base. Several volunteers weighing about 350 pounds took solo rides in the capsule while sensors recorded the pressure created by the occupant's pushing and pulling on the security bar. The riders were asked to act as they normally would in a carnival ride of this type and they were not told the purpose of the experiment. These readings produced a baseline of forces exerted by live riders, including three who weighed the same as the woman who died.

Next a 350 pound dummy was placed into the capsule and spun like a carnival rider. About half-way through the timed ride, the security bar snapped. When the experiment was repeated, the bar snapped under the same stress.

The bars had not snapped with live riders in the capsule because live subjects tend to pull and push on the bar, depending on the movement of the ride. But, when 350 pounds of unyielding dead weight slammed against the metal bar, the bar gave way and the dummy fell out.

Experimental results suggested that if the woman had been alive — or aware — while the ride was moving, she likely would not have fallen out. Because she did fall out, like the dummy, she must have been dead weight; the security bar gave way because the woman was already dead.

The defense attorney apparently had been correct. Zippy should not have been found guilty of negligent homicide because the woman likely had been dead before the ride began.

Mrs. Myers and the 4-H members had gone to the Ford Testing Grounds to watch the experiment, discuss the results, and analyze data. They would write up a report for Lou and for Zippy's attorney. They hoped that this new information could be presented to a new judge, who could order a new trial for Zippy, or simply dismiss the charges.

The phone rang in Nicki Nelson's home. "Hello."

"Hi, I'm checking in," a woman's voice remarked.

"You had better lay low for a while longer."

"Why? What's been happening?"

"Bonnie was found shot last evening, that's what!"

"Really? Oh, my gosh."

"Yeah, just terrible," Nicki replied. "I haven't a clue as to who did it."

"I wouldn't know, either. Have I been mentioned in regard to Win's murder?"

"I've not heard mention of you as a suspect by name, or even as someone seen at the fair that night."

"Good. I like to hear that. Listen, I'm going to stay low for the time being. I'll call you in a few days. Please keep your eyes and ears open for me."

"Okay, will do."

Jack talked with Sheriff Lloyd about getting TV coverage on WLNS-TV's CrimeStoppers to show an image of the unbalanced scales tattoo. The sheriff was okay with the idea and contacted the station, which agreed to cooperate. All the producer needed was an approximation of the tattoo.

Together, Lou and Kristen Cook of The Pampered Chef came up with a drawing that would do, and Lou faxed it to the TV station. That evening those watching the six and eleven o'clock news broadcasts would hear news anchor Sherry Simpson say: "If anyone has seen a tattoo like the one shown on the screen, please contact the CrimeStoppers 800 number. The tattoo, with little if any color, may appear on the mid to lower calf of a woman's right leg. Police are seeking the bearer of this tattoo in conjunction with a high-profile crime."

About 7:30 p.m., Lou received a call from the producer at WLNS-TV. "Well, we got some responses to your tattoo piece. Many said the judge's wife has a tattoo like that, which you already know. Others simply said they knew someone with a tattoo above the ankle, but they couldn't be certain what the design was. We'll air the same request following the eleven o'clock news. Shall I call if anyone responds then, or shall I wait till morning?"

"I want to know as soon as possible. Don't hesitate to call and if I don't answer, please leave a message."

"Okay, will do. Hope this helps."

Denny had set up a code with Zippy Roelof to report on his promise to get revenge against Judge Breckinridge. If Zippy received a letter from Denny asking for a loan, it meant the judge was dead. If Denny sent a letter about a death in the family, it meant he was still working on a plan.

The two men knew that mail would be opened and perhaps read, especially if it came from someone who had been recently released from the penitentiary. The two decided that a request for money or word of a family death should not raise suspicion, and it didn't.

Zippy took the letter from the envelope and read, "Hope you are doing okay. If you got any cash, I could use a loan. Let me know."

Zippy took a deep breath and relaxed completely. If he had to spend years cooped up in a hole, at least the man who put him there wasn't around to enjoy the better things of life, either. Zippy smiled, folded the letter, and repeated softly, "Thank you, Denny. Thank you, Denny!"

Because CrimeStoppers aired during the eleven o'clock news, Lou watched a Detroit Tigers game to stay awake. Normally, the pace of the game lulled him to sleep, but this was a pitchers' duel, and the Tigers pitcher, Justin Verlander, had a no-hitter going as he entered the ninth inning.

When the phone rang at 11:50, Lou answered.

"Lou, we received more calls on the tattoo," the producer reported.

"I was hoping for that," Lou replied.

"One caller said the tattoo resembled one a group of college women were required to get as part of an initiation."

"That's odd. And the others?"

"They all mentioned Bonnie Breckinridge's tattoo, but again, some were uncertain of the design. The caller about the college initiation described female students at a college around Lansing. They were rejected as pledges to a prestigious sorority or something. Or maybe it was an activist group seeking justice for inequities they discovered in the legal system. Anyway, a tattoo was required to join another society. The tattoo seemed to symbolize sacrifice, enduring physical pain to represent the emotional pain of rejection. The unbalanced scale of justice was a visual representation of the injustice these women felt."

"Really," Lou replied, taking notes.

"Apparently, it was their way of getting back at the snobs. It also let people on campus know that a group that supposedly worked for justice followed an elitist policy, enforcing their own style of injustice."

"Interesting."

"Yeah. The caller wasn't sure of the college, the name of the group, or how many got the tattoo."

"Did it appear the caller was one of the women associated with this rejected group?"

"No, the caller was male."

"Did he leave a name or number?" Lou asked.

"No. CrimeStoppers' success is based on a policy of not needing to leave a name or number. Some people do, but this person did not."

"But surely, you can trace calls or use caller ID to find the number of the last caller," Lou reasoned.

"We don't."

"But, don't you need some way to contact people to arrange for the reward if their tips lead to the arrest and conviction of a criminal?" Lou asked.

"You're right. There is a system, but we don't allow anyone, including the police, to access that. This is a tip-line, and its success depends on confidentiality."

"Okay. I understand. I appreciate the lead. I expect that Sheriff Lloyd is aware of this tip?"

"Yes."

"If you get any other calls, please let me know."

"Certainly, Lou."

Lou called Heather the morning of August 16. "I've a job for you, Heather, if you have the time."

"I always have time, Mr. Searing."

"Thank you. We received a lead with a story behind it. During the 1980s, a group of college women sought justice when, by their perception, an injustice occurred in the court system. This was an elitist group. Others formed a counter-group. It was made up of women denied acceptance by the elitist group. The rejected women, banding together, insisted their members get a tattoo of the unbalanced scales of justice. The imbalance represented not only injustice against someone in court, but also the injustice of their not being allowed to join the elitist group. I need you to find out about these tattooed women."

"Thanks for the assignment," Heather replied. "I'll try not to let you down."

Heather immediately contacted the Dean of the College of Law at Michigan State University, thinking he or she would know about the rejected women if they did in fact join together in the 1980s. After a lengthy explanation of who she was and what she needed, Heather's call was put through to Dean Lenore Coscarelli. Heather introduced herself and explained the reason for her call. She then related the story behind the tattoo. After a ten-second pause, Dean Coscarelli responded. "A group like you describe formed at a law school in Lansing. They were excellent students. For some women who were not accepted, it was 'ho-hum', but for others, the rejection was devastating. I recall that some sort of tattoo was a part of the initiation into this secondary body of rejected women. At that time, the early to mid-1980s, getting a tattoo was not nearly as common as it is today, so it was quite a statement."

"Do you know anyone who was a member of this group?" Heather asked.

"I'm sorry, I don't. None of my students were part of it. I only know the group existed. I'm afraid I can't be of more help."

"On the contrary," Heather replied. "You've been very helpful, and I appreciate your time."

A review of Bonnie's computer contents, files, and personal papers gave no clue to a tattoo or anything else relevant to Win's murder. The computer's hard drive had been taken by the state police for an analysis of deleted items and visits to Internet web sites. Lou was disappointed, but it looked as if Bonnie had expected she would be killed and had made sure authorities would find nothing to implicate her in her husband's murder.

Lou had also visited Kristen Cook of The Pampered Chef to see if Bonnie might have been the woman at the Republican booth the night of the murder. Kristin looked at Bonnie's photo and quickly said, "No, this woman is much heavier than the woman I saw."

Heather remained challenged by Lou's request. She contacted Lansing Law College, drove to Lansing from Kalamazoo, and sought out the law library. Then she asked for help in locating any campus newspapers from the early 1980s. An assistant librarian brought her microfilms of *Legally Speaking*, the campus weekly. Heather asked the librarian if he had heard of the counter group, but he had not.

Heather quickly scanned the microfilm dated 1980 and found no mention of an "Outsiders" society. Films from 1981 through 1983 also provided nothing. She was on the verge of giving up when she found an article in the May 1984 edition.

Student Group Aids Victims of Injustice

A new student group has formed at Lansing Law College. The students' stated goal is to seek justice for those who feel it has been denied them through the legal process. Mary Swift, faculty sponsor, and Emily Woosten, club president of Justice Where There Was None (JWTWN) are excited that several students wish to take on the challenges of difficult appeals. They invite women to apply for membership. Miss Woosten made it clear that not everyone who applies will be accepted.

The group meets in the President's Conference Room in Tellon Hall each Tuesday evening at 7 p.m.

Heather scrolled through later 1984 editions for further news, finding another article in the September edition:

Women Join forces,
Free Man Wrongly Convicted of Larceny

The Justice Where There Was None group, or JWTWN, founded last May, reported its first success in bringing justice to those who believed themselves denied it. Larry Bostick was found guilty of larceny in January 1979 and sentenced to seven years in prison. A thorough review of court documents turned up a confession by Ricky Abbott during interrogation for a similar crime in a nearby county. Larry Bostick will be freed from Michigan's Jackson Southern Prison next Thursday. The women plan to celebrate their victory by taking Mr. Bostick and members of his family to dinner.

In the November issue, Heather found the following:

Winston Breckinridge Challenges Women's Group

Winston Breckinridge, a law student at Lansing Law College, has filed a court injunction to stop a campus group, Justice Where There Was None, from meeting. He claims their policy of excluding men from membership is discriminatory and denies him the right to participate in a student activity that should be open to anyone. The matter is being reviewed.

In a related matter, two women who applied to JWTWN for membership and were denied acceptance into the organization plan to challenge membership policies, also.

In the December edition Heather found another report:

Breckinridge Wins, Is Accepted into JWTWN

Winston Breckinridge has won his anti-discrimination claim against the JWTWN. The Law College Board voted to require the group to admit men, but the Board affirmed that the group could deny women membership if applications showed their experience failed to meet group standards. Several women rejected by JWTWN who wish to remain anonymous will continue to fight this decision and may form a separate organization.

After Heather began checking the 1985 microfilm pack, she found an article in the March edition.

Rejected Women Burning Mad

A group of women whose membership applications were rejected by Justice Where There Was None have formed a separate body. Group leader Rita Telman reports that the group currently numbers five. Any woman rejected by JWTWN may automatically become a member if she is willing to display a tattoo above her right ankle. The tattoo, unbalanced scales of justice, represents these women's belief that they were unjustly treated. Unlike JWTWN, the new group, Remove Unjust Attorneys or RUN, will seek out corrupt attorneys and attempt to have their license revoked.

Heather found one more reference to the organizations. It appeared in the May 1985 issue.

Breckinridge Takes on RUN

Senior law student Winston Breckinridge, representing the campus organization Justice Where There Was None, is asking the Board of Regents of the Lansing Law College to disband a new women's group, Remove Unjust Attorneys, or RUN. Rita Telman, RUN's leader, welcomed the challenge from JWTWN and Mr. Breckinridge. Rita said, "Win had better keep his nose clean, because if he doesn't, he'll find new meaning in the phrase, 'lawyer on the RUN!'"

Heather found one more mention of RUN in the July 1985 issue.

Breckinridge Wins: Regents Force RUN to Disband

The Lansing Law College Board of Regents has agreed with student Win Breckinridge that the new organization Remove Unjust Attorneys, or RUN, is in conflict with the Bar Association's Code of Ethics and their procedures to police their members. In addition, Breckinridge noted the similarity of the two student groups. The Board of Regents felt that one student advocacy organization was sufficient, citing sorority and fraternity policies of choosing and rejecting membership to be consistent with current case law.

Rita Telman, leader of RUN, said she was disappointed with the ruling and insisted that RUN would appeal the decision. Co-founder Bonnie Watkins was especially angry and threatened Mr. Breckinridge with bodily harm. Lansing Law College's Dean Smithson has informed the board that Miss Watkins' action could result in discipline or dismissal from the college.

Heather quickly scanned later editions for a follow-up story, but found none. She contacted the Registrar for information about Bonnie Watkins but she was denied information on grounds of confidentiality. When Heather persisted, the Registrar finally said, "All I can tell you is that Miss Watkins stopped attending LLC early in 1986."

Heather copied and faxed the articles to Lou, Jack, and Maggie, and each of them read the information with much interest. What Heather had found cleared up several questions and showed the detective team another direction.

Lou called Heather. "Thanks for such excellent work! You get a star in your crown."

"I'm glad you're satisfied, Mr. Searing."

"We still have a lot to do, but my best guess is that the woman at the Republican booth with the tattoo is the person who pulled the trigger. Who else is involved the conspiracy is not clear. But I wanted to pat you on the back for your results!"

"Thank you, sir."

"I wish you would call me Lou," he said warmly.

"Thanks, but I can't do that. I hold you in high regard, and I was raised to address my elders with respect."

"Well, I can't change that, but if it becomes comfortable, it's more than okay for you to call me 'Lou'."

"Thank you."

eleven

At Lou's request, Maggie was to re-interview attorney MeLissa Evans. Maggie called and the two agreed to meet at Starbucks. Over tea and apple muffins, Maggie began.

"We're making progress in the Judge Breckinridge case."

"Good. I'm glad to hear that."

"We've uncovered information we think will break the case."

"And I presume you think meeting with me will assist you even further."

"That's correct," Maggie replied. "Does an organization known as Justice Where There Was None mean anything to you?"

"Yes, it does. That group formed at Lansing Law College in the mid-1980s. It was a fun bunch, you know, one of those immature activities most young people engage in."

"What made it an 'immature activity'?" Maggie asked.

"Well, first of all, it hurt people. Initially they didn't let men in, and then they barred particular women from becoming members. It was all based on whether they were liked — a popularity contest. Some women took it seriously and were hurt. Others saw it for the immaturity that it was and moved on."

"I take it you were not a member?"

"I *was* a member, but looking back, I'm embarrassed to say I joined the group."

"Was Judge Breckinridge a member?" Maggie asked.

"Not that I was aware of."

"Do you remember Rita Telman being voted down for membership in JWTWN?"

"Yes. She took the rejection personally and very hard."

"Do you know the names of any of the other women who were rejected?"

"Nicki Nelson was rejected, but I don't remember the names of the others."

"Do you know why the rejected women got tattoos?" Maggie asked.

"It was a show of support for each other. I mean, getting a tattoo is painful so it must have shown a deep-seated desire to be a part of something and to demonstrate courage, I suppose."

"You seem quite certain that Judge Breckinridge had nothing to do with the all-female activity," Maggie said.

"I'd certainly know if Win Breckinridge was involved," MeLissa snapped.

"Perhaps this will jog your memory," Maggie brought out the *Legally Speaking* articles and handed them to her.

MeLissa slowly read the articles, took a deep breath, and put her head in her hands. A few seconds later, she sighed and said, "I lied to you, Maggie."

"Why?" Maggie asked.

"It brings back some terrible memories."

"I'm wondering whether there's a connection between the judge's murder and what might have happened in your law school years."

"That's a legitimate question. I'm not sure his murder relates to what happened at the Lansing Law College, but I agree that the motive for his murder may involve some of us at the Lansing Law College."

"Thank you, MeLissa. I'm sure we'll talk again."

Maggie reported her interview to Lou.

"What *is* going *on* here?" Lou asked, shaking his head. "This is crazier than a TV soap opera."

"Maybe MeLissa killed the judge?" Maggie asked. "She lied about the judge's involvement at the Law College."

"Maybe she did kill him. But why have these crazy sorority members stayed in mid-Michigan?" Lou wondered aloud. "I mean we have the judge, his wife Bonnie, Bonnie's friend Nicki, the judge's after-hours visitor MeLissa Evans. And it seems like everyone except the judge has a tattoo on the lower leg."

"Do you know for certain that the judge didn't have a tattoo?" Maggie asked.

"No, I assumed..."

"Not a word you like us to use, Lou," Maggie said smiling. "You'd better get the facts."

Lou called Sheriff Lloyd and asked that Win Breckinridge's autopsy report be forwarded to him; his fax machine printed the report within minutes. Lou read the document carefully, finding no mention of a tattoo. However, on the fax transmittal page Sheriff Lloyd penned the following, "FYI, the nervous lady and her dog reported by Mrs. Norman were visitors from Illinois. You can put that clue to bed, Lou."

twelve

Lou welcomed his evening walk with Carol on the shore. The two took turns pulling Samm in her red Radio Flyer wagon. At one point they stopped and helped Samm out of the wagon so she could sniff the off-shore breeze, attempt to chase a seagull, and feel the cool waters of Lake Michigan against her legs.

"How's the case coming?" Carol asked.

"We're making headway. We may have chased some wild geese for a while, but I think it will come together."

"From what I've overheard, it sounds like a drama is being played out from law school days."

"That's exactly what seems to be happening. We've identified numerous characters, and the single factor tying them together seems to be a tattoo of the unbalanced scales of justice."

Lou and Carol sat on a huge piece of driftwood and pulled Samm's wagon close. They watched sailboats, kites high in the evening sky, and other couples walking hand-in-hand along the shore. They sat still, holding each other's hand, enjoying the lake and its evening activity.

Lou broke the silence when he said, "We had better get Samm back. The sun's starting to go down, and it will get cool."

As Carol started to get up, she remarked, "I think this entire tattoo and college law school business is a cover-up. I think the crime has nothing to do with college, or with body art."

Lou hung on her words; Carol said little about his cases, but occasionally she brought a new aspect that seemed to make sense.

"Explain your thinking, please."

Carol petted Samm while she looked across the water. "As you say, it's a soap opera involving people and events from twenty years ago. People hold grudges, but they also move on. I'm not saying their law school experiences and tattoos are not critical to solving your case. My point is that I think the event triggering the judge's murder occurred fairly recently; the murder was likely premeditated, and it may involve a conspiracy. I'll be curious to see if my thinking is on or way off-base."

"You raise an interesting point. I'll pursue it."

The two stood up, turned Samm's red wagon around, and walked along the beach toward their home.

Lou called Jack and shared Carol's perceptions.

"You know, I think she may be right," Jack replied.

"Maybe we've been lulled into thinking the murderer is the tattooed woman."

"I've had similar thoughts, but didn't say anything, which isn't like me," Jack admitted.

"We definitely need to identify the tattooed woman at the Republican booth the night of the murder, but a motive now seems more important."

"Anything I can do, Lou?" Jack asked.

"Yes, contact Denny Daly and find out about his relationship, if any, to the judge."

Jack was able to contact Denny quickly. They would meet in Charley's Restaurant in Imlay City as soon as Denny got out of work.

Denny began. "Are you close to solving this case?"

"Not really," Jack replied. "There are a lot of characters in this drama."

"I'll bet."

"Denny, I need you to tell me the truth. What do you know about this mess?"

"Judge Breckinridge put my buddy, Zip, in prison. It was wrong — a mistake, a huge mistake. Zip asked me to get revenge for him when I got out. I promised him I would. But, then I realized I was getting a fresh start, and I didn't want to do anything that would put me back in prison. I had to save face with Zip, so I sent him a coded note to let him know that the judge was dead."

"Did you kill the judge, Denny?" Jack asked.

"Absolutely not! When I heard he had been murdered, a wave of relief came over me like I've never felt before. Now I could report that he was dead without having anything to do with the murder. I've never felt so relieved."

"Do you know who might have killed the judge?"

"Sorry, I don't."

"How about Zippy's wife?" Jack asked.

"Didn't happen. Zip would have told me if she did."

"Maybe he didn't know?" Jack asked.

"The family was upset at the judge, and that's a fact. But Zip's wife couldn't kill someone over the mistake."

"Remember, friends and families are often shocked when they learn a person they thought innocent is a killer!"

"I know that, but she didn't kill the judge, Mr. Kelly. Trust me. I can help you clear your list of suspects by erasing two: you can take me off, and you can erase Zip. Keep asking your questions, but the fact is, we're both innocent of the murder."

"Thanks for talking with me, Denny."

"Not a problem."

While Jack talked with Denny, Lou contacted Bonnie Breckin-ridge's friend, Nicki Nelson, who agreed to see him. When they met, Lou quickly looked for the tattoo above her right ankle and sure enough, there it was.

"I knew you would come knocking sooner or later," Nicki said, after shaking Lou's hand.

"This may not be polite, but if you thought that, why didn't you seek me out? I'd like to hear what you know and what you think I should know."

"Fear, I suppose," Nicki replied immediately. "I've seen many television crime shows, how people who might have information are treated. They aren't believed, and the detectives try to get them to say things that may not be true just to fit their theories. At least, that's how I look at it. So, why would I want to bring stress on myself? I've got enough already."

"Good answer," Lou replied. "I can't blame you for waiting for me to come to you."

"Well, you're here, so what questions do you have? Let me say right off the bat, I did not kill the judge. You can think whatever you want, but no evidence will point to me as his killer."

"Well, we're looking for a woman with an unbalanced set of scales tattoo above her right ankle, because we think she may have pulled the trigger. If you've a tattoo at the base of your right leg, you're right up there on my list of suspects."

"Well, I guess that means I'm high on the list."

"First, what's the story behind the tattoo?" Lou asked.

"You'll probably find out about it, but back in the mid-1980s in Lansing, a group of women formed an all female society to fight injustice. But some women were excluded. As often happens, those who were rejected formed a group of their own. I was one of those rejected, and I became a member of the new group. It was required that we get a tattoo of unbalanced scales."

"A painful initiation, if you ask me," Lou said.

"I guess so. I suppose it ranks up there with what fraternities were doing to pledges at the time. But we were young and carefree and immature, so it seemed to fit. Like a gang symbol, it marked us as members of a society out to save the world. We called it RUN, for Removing Unjust Attorneys. So, that's the story behind the tattoo."

"How did you get an acronym of RUN, when 'N' doesn't represent the word 'attorneys'?"

"I don't know. We liked the acronym is all."

"Where did you get the tattoos?"

"An artist at Punch's Parlor gave us a good rate." Lou noted the name of the place in his notebook.

"And Bonnie Breckinridge was also a member?" Lou asked.

"Correct."

"What role, if any, did Win Breckinridge play in this?" Lou asked.

"Winston was a strange actor in the drama. He challenged the idea that an all-woman group should exist, and he won. Then he fought to destroy our group, RUN, and he managed that. Around that time he was also suspected of sexual abuse, but that was just a vicious rumor — it wasn't true."

"Are you sure?"

"I was with Bonnie when she suggested the charge be leveled against him."

"And those two got *married*?" Lou asked, already knowing the answer.

"Well, love is love. They came to realize that they both wanted justice, as they each defined it, and from that shared passion came a relationship that ended in marriage."

"You mean began their marriage," Lou corrected Nicki.

"No, I meant what I said; it *ended* with their marriage. They despised each other. I'm not sure they ever consummated their marriage."

"Why didn't they divorce?" Lou asked.

"An excellent question! It defies logic, is all I can say."

"Tell me about MeLissa Evans," Lou said.

"MeLissa Evans was the judge's mistress. Or at least that is what a lot of people believe. If you didn't know this, I'd be shocked. Certainly it's public knowledge."

"How did Win get elected?" Lou asked.

"The same way *anyone* gets elected — favors and promises. His opponents were all weak. In any other region he'd have come in last with mud all over his glasses, but in this county he was seen as some sort of god."

"I assume Evans is from Lansing Law College, also. Was she or wasn't she a member of the elitist organization?"

"She was in the elitist group."

"Why did so many people from Lansing Law College remain in mid-Michigan after graduation?" Lou asked.

"When we were in Lansing, we studied hard and we played hard. We liked Big Ten sports, the culture at MSU and in local restaurants and bars. So, as we neared graduation, it was a no-brainer to look for jobs in the Lansing area. Some of the friends stayed friendly, and others went separate ways."

"Did the judge and attorney Evans care about rumors of their infidelity?" Lou asked.

"Oh, sure, they cared. But as rumors began to fly, they simply denied them, saying they were nasty rumors spread by small-minded people."

"Let me get to the point," Lou said.

"I was wondering when you'd say that," Nicki interrupted, "so, let me beat you to the answer. I have an idea who killed the judge *and* Bonnie, but I have no evidence."

"We'll try to find the evidence," Lou replied. "Please tell me your idea."

"I think the murderer is Colon Manley. Everyone believes the judge fired a rifle into Colon's bedroom, at a shadow he thought was Colon. I imagine it would be difficult to go through life wondering when a shot could come from behind any object and end your life. My brother coached high school football, and I remember him saying countless times, 'The best defense is a good offense.' I think Colon simply went on the offensive and removed the fear that his life could end at any moment."

"That makes sense. But how do you account for the woman with the tattoo being near the booth and the judge seconds before the fatal shot was fired?" Lou asked.

"I *can't* account for it."

"Let me put it this way. Can you give me the names of the women who have the tattoo?"

"I can tell you those I know."

"That's fine."

"Bonnie, Janie Walker, Alice Jamison, Tommi Haynne, and me."

"What can you tell me about these women?"

"Alice could be your murderer. She's volatile, feisty, and may even be bi-polar. Other than Win's voting to keep her out of JWTWN, I wouldn't know of a motive. She has a couple of teen-aged boys, so she's dealing with all the issues encountered by mothers of teenagers."

"And Tommi?"

"She lived in Dansville for a year or two, and then decided the winters were not her cup of tea and moved to Florida. I don't think she's involved in this. She's seeing some guy named Peter, but I don't know anything about him."

"And Janie Walker?" Lou asked.

"She married Lester Grant, but she kept her maiden name. She wouldn't kill the judge. It's not in her nature."

"Thank you, Nicki."

"Can I trust you won't tell Alice I pointed you in her direction?" Nicki asked.

"Yes, you can trust me. If you think of something else that might help us solve this murder, please give me a call. Here's my card."

Within ten minutes, Lou placed a call to Kristen Cook of Pampered Chef. "I have another description that might fit the tattooed woman you saw the night of the murder. This woman is tall, skinny, and blonde."

"Nope. The woman I saw wasn't any of those — medium height, medium build, and brown hair."

"Okay, thanks, just checking."

The second call was one made by Nicki. "Well, the authorities are looking for the woman with the tattoo seen at the Republican booth before the judge was murdered."

"I knew it! I don't know what I was thinking wearing that skirt to the fair. It was hot that evening, so I didn't want to wear slacks. But such a stupid mistake may put me in the slammer."

"Just thought you'd want to know. They know the woman was not Bonnie, and she wasn't me, either."

"Terrible news, but yeah, I did want to know. Thanks for calling."

"Take care of yourself, Artie."

Heather was college-age and Alice had teenagers, so Lou asked Heather to see what she could learn about Alice and her family. A meeting was arranged at Alice's home in Okemos.

"Thanks for seeing me, Mrs. Jamison," Heather began.

"Alice, please. Let's not stand on ceremony."

"As I told you, I'm working with Lou Searing, investigating the murder of Judge Breckinridge."

"Yes. It's very sad that Bonnie was also killed."

"You knew Win and Bonnie, correct?" Heather asked.

"Yes, we went to law school together in Lansing."

"I see you have a tattoo," Heather said. "I'm thinking of getting one."

"It was a part of a ritual back in the 1980s, and I've regretted it every day since the artist put it on," Alice explained. "I'd rather not talk about it, if that's okay with you."

"Sure. I was just curious. Seems everyone has a tattoo these days."

"Just make sure it's something you're willing to live with the rest of your life."

"Good advice. Have you any idea who might have killed the judge?" Heather asked.

"That's a question I should be asking you. I'm sure your investigative team has uncovered a large cast of characters. I'm not sure I could add anyone you haven't identified. No, I don't know who killed Win. He had a lot of problems, though, made some poor decisions in his personal and professional life. I heard a rumor that he shot at a man. That's very scary, but it's just a rumor. I really have no idea who killed Win."

"Did you go to the county fair this year?"

"Yes, I did, as a matter of fact," Alice admitted.

"You like fairs? Is that why you went?" Heather asked.

"One of my sons was there to show animals for a friend who lives on a farm. I wanted to support him, so I went with him."

"What are the names of your sons?"

"The oldest is Noah. He's seventeen. He's the one who went to the fair with me. My younger son is Isaac, who's thirteen."

"Biblical names, I see."

"Turns out they are, but their father liked the names. People think they, or we, are Jewish, but we aren't. The kids take some ribbing because of their names, but they handle it well."

"You mentioned their father. What is his name?"

"We're separated at the moment. His name is Peter. He's a good father. He drives for UPS."

"How are the boys doing, Alice?" Heather asked.

"Oh, you know, okay, I guess. They're typical teenagers, rebellious, think they know what's best for them. I'm the enemy — authoritarian. I'm in the way of their freedom. I suspect they're experimenting with drugs, so I'm being extra cautious and nosy."

"It's a difficult time for parents and teens."

"You know, if it weren't for the Big Brother/Big Sister program, I don't know what I would do. Judge Breckinridge was Noah's Big Brother, and he did a great job, filling the void of not having a father to talk to and do things with."

"How is Noah taking the judge's murder?" Heather asked.

"Okay, I think. He seemed relieved that there would be no funeral or memorial service. He told me, 'That would have been hard to go to,' so my guess is that he's taking it kind of hard. He hasn't talked much about it. I think football has gotten most of his attention lately."

"The night you went to the fair, did you spend any time near the Republican booth in the commercial building?"

"I was all over the place, but I don't recall spending any time there. I do recall seeing some businesses in a couple of buildings, so I probably was near it."

"Did you stop, review any election material, or talk with anyone in the booth?" Heather asked.

"Yes, I did, now that you mention it. It was late in the afternoon, and I was to meet Noah about five o'clock at the bingo tent. When he wasn't there at five, I wandered a bit, and I think that's when I stopped at the Republican booth."

"Were you at the fair during the blackout?"

"No. I was at home."

"And your sons — were they home?"

"No, they have a summer curfew of 11:30 p.m. I think they were out with friends."

"What about your ex? Did he go to the fair?"

"I have no idea."

"You didn't see him there, then?"

"That's right. You know, it's odd that of the thousands of people at the county fair, I saw only one person I knew."

"Who was that?" Heather asked.

"MeLissa Evans."

Following the interview with Alice, Heather spoke with her older son, Noah.

"I was able to learn a lot from your mother so I won't repeat my questions. But please tell me if what I say is true: you were at the fair on August 8 to show a friend's animals; your Big Brother was Judge Breckinridge; and you weren't at the fair when the blackout occurred."

"All of that's true."

"Do you know who killed the judge?" Heather asked.

"No."

"Did you see anyone you knew at the fair that afternoon?"

'Tons of people."

"School friends?" Heather asked assuming Noah's response.

"Yes, and neighbors, and my father."

"Your father was there?"

"He was at work, delivering a package to the fair office."

"Did you talk to him?"

"Yes. I talked to him over by his truck."

"What did he say?"

"He said he was glad to see me, and that he had to get going because he had a lot of packages to deliver. He asked me if I was going to be at the fair later that night. I told him no. He said he was coming back, if he had any energy left from a long day."

"Have you seen him since the fair?"

"No."

"Do you know if he returned to the fair that evening?"

"One of my friends told me he saw him bidding on a chainsaw carving of a bear standing on his hind legs. I understand he got it."

"Your mom said Judge Breckinridge was your Big Brother in that program."

"Yes. Once a week he took me to dinner or maybe to a Lugnuts game, or in winter to an MSU basketball or hockey game. I liked that. He had two season tickets to all the major Michigan State sports. Most of the time we went to a sports event and had something to eat."

"Did he ever discuss any problems?"

"I don't think so."

"Never mentioned that he feared anyone?" Heather asked.

"Not that I can remember."

"Thanks for talking with me, Noah," Heather said.

"You're welcome."

Isaac was at soccer practice. Heather decided that he wasn't involved in this drama so she decided not to talk with him.

thirteen

AUGUST 19TH

Lou contacted Zippy by phone at the Lapeer Prison. "I've good news. A group of 4-H Club members from Rives Junction, with the help of Michigan State University professors, have proven that the security rail on the Egg-Beater gives way when strained by a mass of 350 pounds. Live people use the security bar as a support, and they often pull it in toward them while the ride is operating. But a dead weight forces the bar out, and it buckles.

"Your attorney can use these findings for an appeal. I think this is evidence, if not proof, that the woman was dead when the ride started. You can't be responsible for killing someone who is already dead."

"Thanks, Lou. Maybe this will reverse the case," Zippy replied, breathing deeply like a weight had just fallen from his shoulders.

"I think it will."

"Too bad that poor excuse for a judge isn't around to feel the pain he caused me."

"I understand your feelings," Lou replied.

"But him being dead takes care of that pain."

As Lou listened to Zippy's anger, he had the feeling Zippy may have been involved in the murder. Lou asked point-blank, "Did you kill the judge?"

"Kill him?" Zippy asked sarcastically. "Maybe you didn't notice I'm locked in this place 24/7 so I was here when he was shot."

"I realize that. But, you could have hired a hit-man."

"Right. Like I've got money to pay someone to kill somebody — that costs a bit more than $10.95."

"Maybe you befriended someone who promised to kill the judge for you," Lou suggested.

"Denny didn't kill the judge."

'Denny?" Lou asked.

Zippy looked chagrined. "A guy I knew in this place. We were buddies, and he felt sorry for me. You might think he killed the judge, but he didn't do it."

"Did he *tell* you he didn't?" Lou asked.

"No, but I *know* he didn't."

"The only way you'd know he didn't kill the judge would be if you knew who did. Do you know, Zippy?"

"No, I don't."

"Denny wasn't on my list of suspects, but maybe he should be. I'll talk to him now. But, I knew you would want to hear about the test results — you might be a free man soon."

"I appreciate it, Mr. Searing."

Next, Lou wanted to talk to Wilma Simmons, Executive Director of the domestic union, who was rumored to have sold a number of favors. Wilma was a sophisticated lady who appeared to be a shrewd businesswoman. She drove a Lexus, dressed in fashionable attire, and moved with an elegant air about her.

A secretary escorted Lou into Wilma's office/conference room in a downtown Lansing building. Wilma invited him to a seat at the table.

"Mr. Searing, it's my pleasure to make your acquaintance. I've read your books, and I marvel at your ability to solve a complex case."

"Thank you, but the credit really goes to those who work with me — with a dose of good luck. They have a talent for being in the right place at the right time."

"I see that you enjoy giving credit where credit is due," Wilma said with a smile.

"Just being honest," Lou replied.

"I can't imagine why you wanted to talk to me, but I'm certainly curious," Wilma said taking a seat across from Lou.

"You have the reputation of getting things done."

"Thank you, I think. I have that reputation, and I do accomplish what I set out to do. But what does this have to do with murder?" Wilma asked.

"Your reputation includes the belief that you are the person to contact if someone wants a sticky or difficult situation resolved."

"That's also true, and I thank you for the compliment. But what am I missing? I still don't see any connection to your investigation of a hideous crime."

"I'm about to offend you, and I apologize. I don't know any way to proceed other than to ask outright: Did you have anything to do with the murder of Judge Breckinridge?"

"And, likewise, I don't know any other way to explain than to answer you directly: No, I had nothing to do with the judge's murder."

"Good, that's settled. Now, do you have any idea who may have committed this crime?" Lou asked.

"Oh, yes. But, you have come to those conclusions yourself," Wilma replied. "I can give you my theories if you'd like, given the respect I hold for you. But, I would be surprised if you haven't already explored all of them."

"Thanks for the compliment, but please give me your list," Lou remarked.

"Colon Manley: revenge for the judge's attempt to kill him. His wife, Bonnie: payback for a terrible marriage. Lester Grant: to get the judge off the ballot. Zippy Roelof: revenge for sending him to the pen for killing someone who was already dead. There, how did I do?"

"Not bad."

Lou's goal had been to meet Wilma, observe her demeanor, and to talk briefly with her, not to conduct a detailed interview. So, after the brief chat, he thanked Wilma and left her office.

Maggie noted that Tommi Haynne had been summarily dismissed as a suspect because she lived in Florida. For no particular reason, Tommi had not been considered important. But Maggie had a hunch Tommi might be a player and merited more than a telephone interview. She convinced Lou that Heather should fly to Florida and interview Tommi personally. Lou passed the request along to the sheriff, who agreed to bear the expense.

Two days later Heather sat across from Tommi Haynne in an air-conditioned lounge at Miami International Airport.

"Thank you for meeting with me," Heather offered, beginning the conversation. "I wish this was February instead of August but…"

Tommi interrupted her. "I'm pretty busy. I've got to get back to work," Tommi replied, obviously perturbed at wasting time with this kid from Michigan.

Noting Tommi's negative tone and lack of hospitality, Heather decided to change the subject. Tommi's right ankle seemed bruised and blotched. "Looks like you've been trying to get rid of the tattoo on your leg," Heather said.

"Can't say that's any business of yours," Tommi responded sharply.

"You lived in Dansville for a year before moving here, right?"

"You came all the way down here just to ask stupid questions? Why are you wasting my time?" Tommi sputtered. She began to tap her foot impatiently.

"Did you kill Judge Breckinridge?" Heather asked bluntly.

The foot-tapping eased, and Tommi smiled. "Now we're getting a little meat on the bone. No, I didn't kill him, but if I did, I sure wouldn't admit it to some amateur detective."

"Look, if you cooperate, you can get back to your job. But if you don't want warm and fuzzy, I'll call Miami PD and have you booked on suspicion of murder."

"You wouldn't dare!"

"Is that a challenge?" Heather asked.

Tommi slumped back in her chair. "Okay, ask your cute questions. I'll answer, and then I'll go back to work."

"We already know about you, your Michigan connection, and the people you went to law school with."

"What would you know about my law college experience?" Tommi asked gruffly.

"GPA, 2.9 — I wouldn't hire you to defend a parking ticket. Rejected from a woman's society because people didn't like you; should I be surprised? You only lasted a year at a law firm in Lansing;

your excuse was you didn't like winter, but really you were fired for incompetence. You married a guy named LeRoy, who divorced you for adultery. Need I go on, or is this sufficient?" Heather asked.

"That's sufficient," Tommi answered glumly.

"So, with all your success in school, job, and personal relationships, you're now a suspect in a judge's murder."

"Why would you possibility suspect *me*?" Tommi asked.

"Because Win Breckinridge rejected you as a debate partner at the Lansing Law College; he voted against your membership in JWTWN; and he won several district court cases against you during the year you survived the harsh winter in Michigan."

"OK, I guess you have some reasons, but you missed one."

"That's why I came to Florida," Heather replied, keeping her cool with an effort. "Let's not waste time, Tommi. What can you tell me?"

"I've been seeing Alice's ex, Peter. Win threatened Pete when he accused the judge of offering drugs to his son. I don't like it when someone threatens people I like. Know what I mean?"

"Yes."

"There's a big enough problem with drugs and alcohol. The last person we need pushing that crap is a judge, let alone one who threatened my friend," Tommi replied heatedly.

"So, now do you understand why we wanted to talk to you?" Heather asked.

"I guess so. Sorry I was so uncooperative. Guess I felt threatened."

"Apology accepted. I assume you claim to be innocent?" Heather asked.

"I killed that man a thousand times in my mind, but I did *not* kill him at the fair."

"How about Peter? Did he kill the judge?" Heather asked.

"You're talking to the wrong person. Much as I like him and am thankful he's my friend, Pete will have to answer your question. I can't."

"I'll let you get back to work," Heather said, gathering her notes. "Oh, one more question: why are you having the tattoo removed?"

"I'm sick and tired of people asking me to explain the unbalanced scales of justice. It brings back bad memories every time I think about it."

"Guess you aren't alone when it comes to regretting a tattoo."

"You're right," Tommi replied. "Good luck with your investigation. I apologize for my attitude." She left Heather to wait in the lounge for her return flight.

The Sunday headline read:

Republicans Choose Binder to Replace Breckinridge

The Republican Party of Ingham County has announced that Brenda Binder has been chosen as their candidate for State Representative, replacing former Circuit Judge Winston Breckinridge. Binder has a distinguished record as a Williamston councilwoman. In the time remaining before the election, Binder hopes citizens will consider her record when making a decision regarding her qualifications for state representative.

Lou informed Jack of the new development. "I suppose if we suspect Lester Grant as a murderer of Breckinridge, we should also suspect this Binder woman."

Brenda Binder welcomed Lou and Jack into her home on the Red Cedar River. "My candidacy has enabled me to meet many interesting people in a short period of time. But never in my wildest dreams did I expect to meet two renowned detectives. What causes you to pay *me* a visit?"

"We talk to many people when we investigate a murder, Mrs. Binder. Most of them can tell us little, if anything, and others provide a lot of information. Since your name will be on the ballot in place of Judge Breckinridge's, we want to be sure that you're in no way involved with this crime."

"I can assure you I'm not involved in the crime. Ask anything you wish, however."

"Do you have a tattoo near your right ankle?"

"No, I don't. Does that make me a suspect?"

"If you had one, yes, it would put you on our list. As personal as my request is, could I see your lower right leg?"

"I think not. You believe I'm lying to you?" Brenda replied.

"I don't think you're lying, but it would remove all doubt if you could show me no tattoo."

"You'll have to take my word. I'll decide whether two strange men can inspect my limbs, and you can't. End of discussion."

"Did you go to the county fair?" Lou asked.

"I wouldn't miss it for the world. I take my grandchildren every year! We see the farm animals, and the youngsters enjoy the kiddy rides. We have a ball! It's the one day of the year they can eat what I call 'fair food'. You know, cotton candy, greasy this, greasy that."

"Did you visit the Republican booth in the South Commercial Building?" Jack asked.

"Certainly! It's my chance to pick up materials to advocate for the Republicans. I get yard signs, pins, bumper stickers, and printed material to give to my Democratic and Independent friends."

Lou and Jack were busy writing while Brenda spoke.

"You two are making me nervous. I'm wondering if my answers to your questions are putting me in a bad light."

"Oh, not necessarily," Lou replied. "We're looking for a woman who has a tattoo on her lower leg, and the fact that you don't have one is certainly in your favor. Obviously, the murderer was at the fair, but not with grandchildren. The person definitely stopped at the Republican booth, but not to pick up yard signs."

Brenda relaxed and smiled. "Wow, you had me worried for a minute."

"Nothing to worry about, Mrs. Binder. I think we have what we need. You don't seem to have had any issues with the judge."

"Oh, believe me, I had issues with Win!"

"You did?" Jack asked.

"Who didn't? The difference is, my issues did not involve murder."

Lou used his cell phone to call Kristen Cook of Pampered Chef, who was glad to hear from him.

"I've been following the case closely, but there has been nothing in the paper about an arrest," Kristen said.

"No, we're still gathering information. When the solution isn't obvious, it takes interviewing, researching facts, and finding new leads to trip the spring on the mousetrap. We've several suspects, but we're not ready to have anyone arrested."

"You'll solve it."

"Yes, I expect we will."

"Do you have a question for me, or did you want to purchase something from Pampered Chef?"

"No, that's Carol's role, and she does like several products in your line. But one thought keeps coming up, so I decided to get to the root of it."

"I'll help if I can."

"Could the tattoo you saw have been an image of something other than unbalanced scales of justice?"

After a pause, Kristen replied, "I'm pretty sure it was scales of justice."

"I know you are. But could it have been something else: a butterfly, flowers, or something small with a similar shape?"

"Well, maybe."

"You took a glance, it wasn't good light, and you were at least ten feet away."

"You're right about that."

"I'm not trying to confuse you or plant seeds of doubt," Lou said. "I'm looking for your reaction, something between 'I'm absolutely certain of what I saw' and 'I suppose it *could* have been something else.'"

"In all honesty, I could go with the latter, but I could pass a lie detector test if I answered 'yes' to whether the tattoo was of the unbalanced scales."

"I understand. Thanks, Kristen. I may talk with you again."

Lou called Jack on his cell. "I've a job for you."

"I'm always at your service."

"I'd like you to talk to Peter Jamison, Alice's estranged husband. He's now dating Tommi Haynne."

"OK, I have my marching orders."

"Remember, he purportedly accused Win Breckinridge of giving drugs to his son, and the judge threatened him in response."

"Yes. All of that's in Heather's suspect profile."

"Call me after you talk with him," Lou requested. "I'll be curious what you learn."

"You don't want to conduct the interview?" Jack asked.

"You should do it because you have a way of relaxing people. I seem to come on a bit strong. Besides, my name may threaten him in a different way."

"I'm on it, Lou."

Six hours later, Jack met Pete Jamison at a Taco Bell near Meridian Mall in Okemos. Jack began, "As I said on the phone, I have some questions about the judge's death on August 8."

Pete took a deep breath. "First, you should understand that I had absolutely no respect for that man. I mean, I had no respect for the way he conducted himself on the bench or in his personal life. I grew up believing that public figures were upstanding citizens and law-abiding people. I was taught to look up to public officials.

This guy turned out to be the negative image of my public servant, so if I speak with rancor, you'll understand."

"I know where you're coming from. All I'm asking for is your honest responses to my questions."

"I'll be honest, Mr. Kelly."

"I understand the judge was active in various community organizations, including Big Brothers/Big Sisters."

"That's true. But I heard a rumor that he was pushing drugs to people, including my son Noah. I became very upset, as anyone would, hearing that kind of thing."

"I think your response was normal."

"I didn't keep my emotions bottled up; I let the rumor get to the police and to the organizations where he was volunteering."

"Their response?"

"They basically said I couldn't be right, that I was spreading a vicious rumor."

"What was the judge's response?"

"He asked to meet with me. He told me I was spreading lies about him, and I could face significant retribution if I didn't stop."

"Who told you he was pushing drugs?" Jack asked.

"Bonnie Breckinridge."

"I see. Did your son tell you he had gotten drugs from the judge?"

"No. But what would you *expect* him to say?"

"I understand you have a friend, Tommi Haynne, who lives in Florida."

"Yes, that's right."

"I imagine you told her of this rumor and how the judge reacted?"

"Absolutely."

"And what was her response?"

"She thought I should act before the judge did."

"Meaning?"

"Kill him before he killed me."

"Did you?"

"No, I did not!"

"The night of the murder, you were at the fair after normal work hours," Jack said looking at his notes.

"That's true. My last delivery was to a customer who had his camper at the fair — it was a special order. I called my supervisor and asked if I could leave the truck on the grounds, then drive it home and back to the depot in the morning. He agreed to it, so that's what I did."

"So, if I understand correctly, after delivering the package, you left your van on fair property."

"Yes."

"Did you go to the commercial building displays?"

"Oh, yes. I like to see what the vendors are selling."

"Did you go to the Republican booth?" Jack asked.

"Yes, and I saw Judge Breckinridge there."

"Did he see you?" Jack asked.

"I don't know. People were milling around."

"Did you see any friends or neighbors?"

"Well, Tommi came with me. My son Isaac joined us."

"Tommi was there? She came from Florida to go to the county fair?" Jack asked, stunned.

"Oh, no, she was already here. She comes up here for a few weeks each summer."

"Were you at the fair when the lights went out?"

"Yes."

"Where were you when that happened?"

"I'm not sure, Mr. Kelly. I know I was at the fair, but I wasn't in the commercial buildings at that time."

"Your truck was parked near the breaker box for the commercial buildings. Was that a coincidence?"

"I guess so. I just parked where I wouldn't cause anyone any trouble and then walked to the fair."

"Thanks for talking with me, Peter."

"You're welcome."

fourteen

AUGUST 21 • MASON, MICHIGAN

Sheriff Lloyd called Lou on his cell. "Something has come up that you should know about."

"I'm all ears."

"We have evidence that MeLissa Evans and her vehicle were in the Breckinridge neighborhood about the time Bonnie was shot."

"Interesting."

"A neighbor, Daisy Brickover, was taking a video of her gardens to send to a friend. As she scanned the flowers along her sidewalk, a woman came into view of the camera. When the neighbor was editing the video after Bonnie was murdered, she noticed the woman walking in the neighborhood. That woman was MeLissa Evans."

"I assume you have a copy of the video?" Lou asked.

"I don't have it yet, but she said she'd give it to me."

"Good," Lou replied. "But doesn't it sound odd that Evans would walk into the neighborhood in broad daylight, where she could easily be seen, if she was going to kill Bonnie?"

"Maybe she wasn't planning to kill Bonnie," Sheriff Lloyd said.

"Maybe. And, perhaps Evans didn't even go to see Bonnie," Lou reasoned. "She could have had any number of reasons to be in the neighborhood."

"Anything's possible, Lou. Anyway, I wanted to make sure you were aware of this."

"Thanks, Sheriff."

"Is your team any closer to solving this case?"

"I think so," Lou replied. "As far as I can tell, we've talked to everyone who might have played a role in the crime. We just need to put all the facts on the table and see if a pattern emerges. I can make a case for many people, but I still don't have the one fact that nails it for me."

"You'll get it."

"Thanks for your confidence."

Although Lou thought the results might not be worth the effort, he contacted the judge's long-time secretary, Elizabeth Andrews, inviting her to join him at the Bob Evans restaurant in west Lansing. Lou didn't want to go to the courthouse, nor did he want the court staff to know that he and Elizabeth were talking.

Over coffee and a slice of pie, Lou began. "How are you and the staff adjusting to the loss of the judge?"

"We're doing better now. For a while we were scared that some crazy person might come to work and start shooting. The sheriff provided extra security officers for a week following the murder."

"I'm sure that was reassuring."

"Yes, it was."

"We have been investigating the murder, talking to several people and gathering information. However, just when we began to think we had learned everything, it dawned on me that we hadn't sought out the judge's staff, which is why I asked to meet you here."

"The staff have noted your absence a few times. Mr. Kelly came soon after the murder to review some case files, of course. But we don't have experience in these matters, so we didn't know whether anyone would interview us. We know nothing about the murder, but we just thought eventually someone would question us."

"Better late than never, I suppose," Lou replied

"As I just said, I don't think I can help, but you must have questions."

"Yes. Jack did come to your offices to read case files, and I believe he talked to someone on the judge's staff, a court recorder, as I recall."

"Yes, he talked to Cindy Markle. But I want to make it clear that Cindy is on her own with her observations. I don't know what she told Mr. Kelly, but you should know she had a long feud with Judge Breckinridge. He gave her a poor evaluation after she had been on the job for a while. I'm no psychologist, but I think she's paranoid thinking the judge deliberately made her life miserable. She was furious when she found out he hadn't recommended to continue her employment. He changed his mind and kept her, but there was bad blood between them, let me tell you! I think the poor evaluation was fair; she made numerous errors in transcriptions, and she was often late for trials. Anyway, Mr. Kelly couldn't have known that."

"So, anything she said should be taken with a grain of salt?" Lou asked.

"Yes, about a half-container of Morton's. I don't know what she told Mr. Kelly but my guess is she mentioned an affair between the judge and MeLissa Evans, which did not happen. She may have spoken of the judge dealing in drugs, which is also untrue. If she said anything about his being jailed as a teenager, that's also not true.

"Lately, Cindy's become obsessed with religion. There's nothing wrong with religion but she forces literature on us, pesters us about whether we've been saved, and quotes the Bible often. She gets bees in her bonnet and starts rumors, and the gossip spreads like a prairie fire. I think she's mentally ill."

"OK. We'll take her behavior into consideration," Lou replied. "How would you explain the judge's after-hour visits with Mrs. Evans?"

"I worked many evenings while she was there. The judge made it clear to all of his staff that he was tutoring Mrs. Evans in courtroom examination techniques."

"And, there's no truth to the drug problem?" Lou asked.

"Heavens, no. He did smoke, and he did drink. He always kept a flask in his desk, but he didn't do drugs. I mean, if that were true, he'd have been before the ethics committee and out of practice in an instant."

"How was his relationship with Mrs. Breckinridge?" Lou asked.

"'Strained' is the best word I can use. I don't think they loved one another. They may have at one time, but for almost a decade, I would say their relationship was not a happy one."

"You mentioned your fear of someone coming in shooting. What procedures did the judge have in place for such an irrational act?"

"A button on his phone rings directly into the sheriff's office and during drills, a security officer was there in less than thirty seconds. We also had access to the button, and the judge told us not to hesitate to push it if any of us thought someone was acting strangely."

"Did he keep a firearm in his office?"

"Yes. It was a pistol or a revolver. I don't know the difference."

"Is it still there?"

"I don't know. His office was locked after the murder, and to my knowledge no one has entered. No, wait, that's not true. A police officer came in one day and took the judge's computer and files of current cases. He may have taken the gun then, but I don't know for sure."

Suddenly Elizabeth smiled. "The judge used to comment about his being in the old west. He often joked, saying his gun held six bullets and he hoped he never had to replace one."

"Is anyone working in the office this evening?" Lou asked.

"Not that I know of."

"I'll ask the sheriff to meet us at the courthouse. I want to see if that revolver is there."

"We can do that," Elizabeth replied.

"I'm about finished for now," Lou said, closing his notebook. "But, I'm still curious about Cindy. What did she do for a living before this job?"

"She doesn't talk much about her past, but I recall her saying she cleaned homes, was a receptionist for a doctor, and worked for a newspaper for a couple of years."

"I may want to talk more about Cindy, but for now, that's all. Please excuse me for a moment, Elizabeth."

Lou used his cell phone to call Sheriff Lloyd.

"Sheriff, this is Lou Searing. I've a favor to ask. I'm at a restaurant on the west side of Lansing, talking with Elizabeth Andrews, Judge Win's secretary. She tells me the judge had a revolver in his office in case of threats to himself or his staff. Can someone meet us at the courthouse and give me access to the judge's office? I'd like to see if the gun is still there."

"It's not there, Lou. We've gone over that office with a fine-toothed comb and believe me, it isn't there."

"Okay, thanks, Sheriff.

Lou explained to Elizabeth that they would not be going to the courthouse. He thanked her for talking with him, paid the bill, and walked Elizabeth out to her car.

fifteen

It was time to call the team together for another meeting of the minds. Maggie suggested they come to her home in Battle Creek. Lou agreed and contacted Jack and Heather to meet the next afternoon.

Maggie, her husband, and daughter, LuLing live in a modest, accessible home in southwest Battle Creek. Heather drove over from Kalamazoo, and Lou and Jack rode together to the Cereal City. At four o'clock in the afternoon, the four began their discussion.

Lou spoke first, "Thank you, Maggie, for having us here. I thought it important to hear one another's thoughts. Each of us has fed information to Heather for her to enter into our suspect file. Thank you, Heather, for keeping this up-to-date.

"I had a major revelation yesterday coming home from meeting with Judge Breckinridge's secretary. You know that I generally believe what people tell me unless I have a reason not to. Said another way, I don't automatically mistrust what I hear. Given my inclination, I'm glad you three are able to quickly process what you hear and judge the merits of those facts.

"I've pursued this investigation believing that Win Breckinridge was having an affair with MeLissa Evans and using drugs. Yesterday, Elizabeth Andrews informed me that those accusations are false. When I learned that, I wondered what other things we believe are lies.

"Finally, we expended considerable effort to find the woman with the scales of justice tattoo, which is good, because I think she is somehow involved. But someone connected with this woman may have actually killed the judge, and that person may or may not have had a tattoo. So, considering all of this, I need to see what you three are thinking about these matters, among others."

"I thought the Pampered Chef saleslady didn't necessarily see unbalanced scales but merely an image that approximated the tipped scales," Maggie added.

"Since we're admitting doubts, here's another," Jack said. "I'm not sure the judge fired a shot intending to kill Colon Manley. A lot can be done to alter photo images. Manley could be trying to frame the judge."

Heather was next. "Maybe Judge Breckinridge was a model citizen, and people with axes to grind are spreading rumors."

"And who is so good with schemes and rumors?" Lou asked, knowing the answer.

"Wilma Simmons," Jack replied. Everyone nodded in agreement.

As if on cue, Lou's cell phone began its rhythmic sound. While Lou reached into his pocket to get the phone, Heather said quietly, "I have a feeling there's another murder."

"Hello," Lou answered.

"Lou, sorry to interrupt your meeting," Carol began. "Joyce Wagner wants to know if you're still planning to go to the Tigers baseball game tomorrow. If you're not, she has someone who could use the ticket."

"I'm planning to go."

"OK, I'll call and tell her. Sorry to interrupt your meeting."

"No bother. I'll be home in a few hours."

"Love you, Lou."

"Love you, too."

Lou looked at Heather. "What were you saying about another murder?"

"I just had a feeling, sort of a *déjà vu.*"

"Maybe the Tigers will murder the White Sox tomorrow, but otherwise your vibrations were moving along a different frequency." Everyone laughed.

Just then the phone rang in Lou's hand. "Hello."

"Sheriff Lloyd, Lou. Another development."

"What now?" Lou asked. "Wait, let me put you on speaker. I'm with my team. I want them to hear what you have to say. Okay, go ahead."

"Elizabeth Andrews has been found dead in her office at the courthouse."

"How was she killed?" Lou asked.

The team members uniformly shook their heads and took deep breaths.

"Looks to be a single shot to the head," Sheriff Lloyd replied. "A para-medic thinks it may be suicide."

"We'll be there as soon as possible."

"Thanks, Lou."

Lou put his phone in his pocket, looked at the team, and said, "I owe you an apology, Heather. Your vibes were right on."

"We need to break this case quickly, if only to stop the carnage," Heather replied.

"Jack and I will go over to Mason presently, but let's go over options first," Lou said.

"That phone call disturbed our train of thought," Maggie said. "I tend to think the strongest suspects could be Peter Jamison and Tommi Haynne. If they didn't commit the murders, the guilty party may be Brenda Binder, who replaced Judge Breckinridge on the Republican ticket."

"Maggie may be right," Jack replied, nodding his head.

Heather added, "The most logical possibilities were MeLissa Evans, Mrs. Breckinridge, and Elizabeth."

"Two of those are dead now," Jack interjected.

"Correct," Heather replied.

"When I interviewed Elizabeth Andrews, she said the judge would hold up his revolver, show that six bullets were in it, and say he hoped he never had to replace one," Lou said.

"Which means that his staff knew he had a gun," Jack summarized. "And, the obvious place to keep it is in his office, and to have access to it, in his desk."

"But, the sheriff said his deputies found no gun in the office," Lou said.

"That missing gun is probably the murder weapon," Jack replied.

"You're right, and since the murder weapon has not been identified, the chances of its being the judge's gun are equal to those of any other gun," Heather reasoned. "So, if the judge's gun is the murder weapon, the judge's staff knew it existed, and that he kept it in his office."

"In that case, Cindy Markle is our prime suspect," Lou replied. "However, my guess is that MeLissa Evans knew of the gun, and for all we know, the judge could have told anyone — Bonnie, friends, attorneys. The list is endless."

"So, do we think MeLissa killed the judge, or all three?" Jack asked.

"It's possible. But, what motive do we have?" Lou asked. "Furthermore, we've just heard that his secretary was murdered. What would be her motive for this?"

"Elizabeth Andrews probably knew something the killer doesn't want to get out," Maggie replied.

"Or maybe she told someone else what she told you, Lou, and that angered the killer," Jack added.

"Could be."

"You've listened to us, Lou. Do you have a theory?" Maggie asked.

"A thought is all. I haven't put the facts into the theory, but my thought makes sense."

Jack said, "We're ready to hear from the Master."

"Okay, I'll take a shot. The killer could be Cindy Markle. She was upset with the judge for giving her a poor work evaluation. She used to clean houses, which means she likely knows Wilma Simmons. Cindy plans the murder at the county fair. She knows the judge will be there because she has access to his schedule. Somehow she arranges for the breaker box to blow at a time she thinks chances are best for the perfect crime, when the judge is alone at the Republican booth. Cindy's confident we have no suspicion of her involvement. Then I interview the judge's secretary, who may have told the staff that we talked, and using poor judgment says something she shared with me. Cindy hears this and can see she needs to kill the secretary."

The three quietly evaluated Lou's scenario. It was a couple of minutes before Jack spoke. "I like it — it makes sense. But, I don't think Cindy fired the shots. I think she may have gone to Wilma with her dilemma."

"Remember, Wilma met with Lester Grant prior to the judge's murder," Heather reminded them.

"That's right!" Jack agreed.

"Maybe Wilma saw problems with the judge. She's not happy that a former union worker was not treated fairly, or she didn't think she was treated fairly. Tied to this could be something Grant told Wilma. The combination of two causes could lead Wilma to kill the judge for a fee."

"Grant paid her?" Heather asks.

"Maybe he did, maybe he didn't," Lou replied. "Even if he did, how do you think Wilma managed the murder?"

"She could get the judge's gun from Cindy," Heather said. "She'd then find a hit-man."

"Or hit-woman," Lou replied. "But who would she get? That's the question. Then, if the theory is right, who shoots Bonnie and why? Is it the Wilma connection, or something unrelated?"

The four quietly contemplated the questions.

"In politics, sometimes a surviving spouse steps in to fill the dead person's role. We saw that with Sonny Bono and a few others. Brenda Binder could have viewed Bonnie as a threat to her candidacy," Jack offered.

"Remember, Bonnie said she was a party to the killing," Heather recalled. "I think the killer feared Bonnie might take over, so he or she needed to knock Bonnie off."

"Okay, enough meeting of minds," Lou said. "Jack and I will see what we can learn in Mason. Everyone keep on thinking, and with luck, things will fit together."

"One more thing before we break up, please," Heather said. "There's a person I put into the computer whom we have not contacted."

"Who could that be?" Lou asked, thinking every possible suspect had been identified.

Heather looked at Lou. "You told me that five women had the 'scales' tattoo. We've not contacted Rita Telman, nor has her name come up in conversation with suspects. Her name appeared in the articles in *Legally Speaking*."

"That's right," Lou admitted. "Okay, Maggie and Jack, you work together, and bring her into the case." Both nodded.

sixteen

MASON, MICHIGAN

On the way to Mason, Lou and Jack continued to think about the case. "So why did Elizabeth Andrews die, Jack?" Lou asked.

"She saw something, heard something, or learned something," Jack replied.

"Okay, what could she have seen?"

"Likely something in the court office."

"What could she have heard?" Lou asked.

"Something someone said in the court office."

"What could she have learned?"

"Again something related to the court office."

"So, what did she know?" Lou asked.

"Who killed the judge, and maybe who killed Bonnie," Jack said.

"Exactly. So, the investigation goes back to the court office. Right?" Lou asked.

"Right."

Late that afternoon, Lou and Jack parked two blocks from the Ingham County Courthouse. Vans from the media, state police crime lab, and other law enforcement vehicles were on the scene, responding to the third murder. As they walked toward the courthouse, Lou pointed out a piece of paper or a card on the bordering lawn. Jack leaned down and picked it up.

"It's a name tag," Jack said. "Whoever this belongs to was attending a conference of some kind."

"What's the name on it, Lou?" Jack asked.

Jack turned the piece of cardstock over. "MeLissa Evans."

"Wasn't she in the Breckinridge neighborhood around the time Bonnie Breckinridge was shot?" Lou asked.

"Yes, I believe so."

"Is this a bit beyond chance?" Lou asked.

"Yes, but all we have is a name tag," Jack replied. "It may have been left here to frame MeLissa, or it could have fallen here a day or two ago, or the wind might have picked it out of a garbage truck."

"You're right. But, this could be a significant piece of evidence if MeLissa was wearing it today. We should have been more careful — shouldn't have handled it, possibly contaminating evidence." Lou realized after the fact that it would have been prudent to mark the area and have the crime scene people put the tag in an evidence bag, but it was too late. He'd hand it to one of the on-scene detectives and suggest he enter it along with other items found in or near the courthouse.

Although it had been four hours since Elizabeth's body had been found, many people had remained in the area designated as a crime scene, within the yellow-taped boundary.

Sheriff Lloyd approached Lou. "Thanks for coming," he said, acknowledging both Lou and Jack.

"Very sorry we haven't solved this yet. Elizabeth might be alive if we had completed our work sooner."

"This has nothing to do with you, Lou," the sheriff said. "This is a complicated mess involving many people, each looking for revenge, either for acts committed, or for some very ugly rumors."

"You're right, Sheriff."

"I'd like you two to look at a partial letter Elizabeth was writing."

Sheriff Lloyd led them into the judicial suite, over to the receiving desk.

"Read that note lying on the desk-top," the sheriff told Lou.

Mr. Searing, I have given much thought to our discussion yes-
terday. In reality, I know much more than I told you. The
judge's murder was expected, feared actually, and was a topic
of conversation among the staff at coffee break and as the
"girls" took walks on their breaks. You'll to be led to believe
that MeLissa Evans committed both crimes, but she did not.
The person who murdered the judge and his wife is…

"For crying out loud, how could this happen?" Jack asked.

"We can't assume that Miss Andrews wrote that letter," Lou
replied. "MeLissa could have written it to throw us off and placed it
on the desk where it would be found."

"Or, Elizabeth may have been forced to write it at gunpoint
before she was shot," the sheriff added. "We'll analyze the note and
perhaps learn who wrote it."

"Am I seeing things, or is the jagged line an approximation of
two letters?" Lou asked.

"I see what you mean, Lou, but it's a stretch of the imagination at
best," Jack replied.

"What do you think, Sheriff?" Lou asked.

"I don't see any letters."

"Please have your technicians make a copy, and I'll highlight
what I think could be Elizabeth telling us who is about to kill her,"
Lou said.

As Lou and Jack left the courthouse, Jack asked, "What do you
make of that name tag on the grass?"

"Well, Jack, two things are at work here. MeLissa may have been
in the area, and her name tag came off. I've worn a million of them in

my career, and those things never seem to stay on. Whether she is involved in Elizabeth's murder is unknown, but it's also possible that MeLissa is being set up. Someone could have planted the name tag to implicate her."

Jack took his phone from his hip cell phone holder and dialed a number.

"Who are you calling?" Lou asked.

"Michigan Bar Association. I'll put this on speaker phone." The receptionist answered and Jack introduced himself and asked, "Can you tell me whether there were any conferences of interest to attorneys in Ingham County today?"

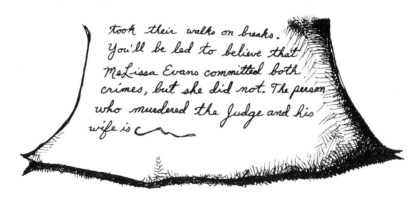

took their walks on breaks. You'll be led to believe that MeLissa Evans committed both crimes, but she did not. The person who murdered the Judge and his wife is

"One moment, please." When the receptionist came back on the line, she said, "We show a seminar titled, 'Computer Crime: Implications for Attorneys,' being held in Holt from ten this morning until two o'clock this afternoon."

"Who would I call for a list of participants?" Jack asked.

"The seminar was sponsored by the law firm of Anderson, Anderson, and Cox. I'll give you their phone number." She recited a local number.

Jack thanked the receptionist and then dialed the law firm. "Good afternoon. I'm Jack Kelly, working with Lou Searing on the murder of Judge Breckinridge. I understand a seminar sponsored by your firm was held in Holt today."

"That's correct," the receptionist replied.

"Was MeLissa Evans registered for the seminar?"

"That would be in my computer. One moment, please. Yes, here's her name."

"Thank you."

Lou dialed his phone.

"I almost said, 'Hi, Mr. Searing.'" MeLissa Evans answered after two rings of her cell phone. "Why am I not surprised to hear from you? I did not kill Elizabeth Andrews, and I don't know who did," she spat. "*And*, the name tag you found in the grass was *not* the one I wore at the seminar!"

"Whoa, whoa, that's too much information too fast," Lou replied.

"Sorry. I've just *had* it with being in your spotlight."

"You're right, we have some questions. But why wouldn't we have, since we found the name tag near the courthouse?"

"I know, I know. The name tag you found is a different style than the ones used at the seminar. Note that it has a printed name on it. At the seminar, each of us was given a tag with our name typed on it."

"Whoa, whoa. How do you know about this found name tag?" Lou asked.

"Let's just say I have friends in law enforcement who thought I should know."

"What do you know about the note Elizabeth was writing when she was shot?" Lou asked.

"Now, I don't know *what* you're talking about," MeLissa replied emphatically.

"Elizabeth appears to have been writing a note to me when she was killed," Lou replied. "The note says you did not murder Judge and Mrs. Breckinridge."

"Well, score a point for me! Guess I'm finally not alone in believing in my innocence!"

"Except that it's possible you held a gun to her head and forced her to write that so that we wouldn't suspect you in any of the murders," Lou rationalized.

"Mr. Searing, give me a break! Why would I kill Elizabeth Andrews?"

"She knew too much. She was close to implicating you, so you had to get her out of the way."

"Oh, sure. That makes a lot of sense. Listen, Lou, you're wasting your time bringing me into focus every time someone is shot."

"Can you help us then?" Lou asked.

"Cindy Markle murdered the judge and his wife. How's that for a definitive statement?" MeLissa asked.

"Give me your reasoning."

"The judge gave her a bad evaluation," MeLissa began. "When she realized he was tutoring me to improve my courtroom skills, she started rumors we were having an affair and that the judge was using drugs. Her revenge was to kill the judge and to point the finger of guilt at me in the process. She killed the judge's wife because Bonnie was a party to the crime and Cindy was afraid Bonnie would let the cat out of the bag. When Cindy heard you were talking to Elizabeth, she had to kill her. Cindy knew the gun was in the judge's desk, and she used it for all three killings."

"You build a strong case and a logical one, at that," Lou replied.

"So, if Mrs. Andrews was writing you a note that says I did not kill either Breckinridge, she knew that's the truth."

"I follow you."

"I can't take much more of this, Lou," MeLissa's tone was softer, followed by a deep breath.

"I imagine you can't," Lou replied sympathetically. "You've given me a good rationale for Cindy as a serious suspect. Let Jack and me follow it and see where it leads."

"Wrap it up, *please.*"

"We'll do our best."

"If you don't, the next body they find most likely will be mine."

"I should have asked you sooner, but now that you are on the line, we have some video that supposedly shows you with a dog walking in Bonnie's neighborhood near the time she was murdered."

"And I thought you were an ace detective, Mr. Searing."

"What is that supposed to mean?" Lou replied.

"That video will have a date on it that appears on tape from all video cameras. You will see August 9. I was in the neighborhood to pay my respects to Bonnie."

"Now that you mention it, I didn't pay attention to any date."

"Oh, my. What can I say?" MeLissa sighed. "I'm sure we'll talk again, Mr. Searing."

Maggie made it her mission to track down Rita Telman, the leader of RUN in the mid-1980s. The Lansing Law College alumni office had a home address in Chicago as well as a summer address in Grosse Pointe. Northeast of downtown Detroit, Grosse Pointe is home to the wealthy, showcasing numerous extravagant residences, most of which have been passed down through several generations. Rita's father, a long-time General Motors engineer, was rumored to have designed Cadillacs in the 1950s.

Maggie drove into Rita's Grosse Pointe neighborhood. Maggie didn't find her at home, so she cruised the area looking for neighbors. She was able to get the attention of a couple sitting on a deck two homes to the east of the Telman estate. Not wanting to exit her car, she motioned for someone to come to her.

"Can I help you?" a middle-aged woman asked as she approached.

"I'm Maggie McMillan, and I'm looking for Rita Telman, but she doesn't appear to be home. I use a wheelchair which is why I asked you to come to me. Thank you."

"That's not a problem. Well, I don't know Rita well — she keeps to herself. But now that you mention it, I haven't seen her for several days. She lives in Chicago, so maybe she's there. Summer people come and go."

"Is she married?"

"I don't know if I should be answering these questions from a stranger, but no, she is not."

"Can you help me find a photo of her? Does the community have a photo directory, for example?"

"We have a directory, but without photos," the woman said.

"I see."

"Wait a minute — we had a neighborhood picnic a year ago, and my husband took several pictures. If you'll wait, I'll ask him. He can put his finger on them within a minute. Pull into our drive, and I'll be right back."

True to her word, a minute later the woman returned with a photo of Rita speaking with a male friend. "My husband says you can have this if you want it."

"Thank you very much," Maggie said, looking at details in the photograph. "Is this Rita's dog?" Maggie asked pointing to a small cocker spaniel.

"Yes, that's Cocoa. She goes wherever Rita goes. We often comment behind her back that Cocoa might as well be her seeing-eye dog."

"And, the man she is talking to — who is he?"

"He's just one of the neighbors, Paul Granger."

"This photo may be very helpful," Maggie said.

"When I see Rita, may I tell her who was looking for her?" the woman asked.

"I'll give you my card, and yes, you can tell her I was looking for her. You could also ask her to call me."

"Be glad to."

"Thank you very much," Maggie said, handing the woman her card.

As Maggie pulled away, the lady looked at the card; when she read, "Maggie McMillan, Private Detective," a shot of adrenaline entered her system, for what she had long suspected had proven true.

seventeen

AUGUST 26TH

For the first time in ten cases, Lou Searing was dumbfounded. Lou said to Jack, "I think we're stumped! And, I think this is the first time that I've really been stymied. We have several scenarios. I can see the murderer as Cindy Markle, Colon Manley, Lester Grant, or Brenda Binder. Everyone has a motive, and anyone could have pulled the trigger or aided in the killings. The only one who has admitted involvement is Bonnie Breckinridge — and she's *dead*."

"We might need to let this one rest a while, Lou," Jack suggested.

"We don't take rests, Jack. Once I take on a case, it's solved. Granted, I've been lucky often, and you, Maggie, and Heather have been instrumental in the solutions. But each has been solved in a relatively short period of time."

"Nine out of ten is a pretty good batting average. I don't know a Detroit Tiger who'd complain about batting nine hundred."

"Yes, but we aren't playing a game. We're resolving people's injustices toward others."

"As is the case with this one, Lou. But, we may well need a break, is all I'm saying. There's no harm or dishonor in that. Some tough murders aren't solved for years."

"Yes, but not one that I've been called on to solve."

Lou took out his cell phone, and placed a call.

"Sheriff, this is Lou Searing."

"Everything okay, Lou?"

"Yes, but my team is at a dead end. Every time we think we're on to a solution, something either diverts our attention or convinces us that we're pursuing a wild goose. We're going to take a hiatus while our minds clear."

"Makes a lot of sense to me, Lou," Sheriff Lloyd replied. "We've nothing new either."

"I hope you'll contact me if you get a new lead. I don't want to give the appearance that we're off the case; we're simply taking a break. The case will be on our minds till it is solved."

"Not a problem. I'll call with any leads."

"Thanks," Lou said.

"And our thanks to you and your team, Lou."

Lou hung up and called Maggie.

"Maggie, we'll be taking a breather in this investigation. I'm tired, stymied, frustrated. So, I'm calling the troops in for a few days until we're refreshed. Sometimes when you come back to a crossword puzzle, the answers are clearer and you move right through the clues. I'm hoping the same thing happens with our case."

"I think that's a wise decision, Lou. I'll let Heather know, and we'll wait for your call."

"Thank you Maggie. And please be sure to thank Heather for me. You two are doing a great job."

"While you're on the line, I have something for you. I wasn't able to talk with Rita Telman, but I did get a photo of her. You might want to show it to Kristen Cook. Rita could be the woman with the tattoo at the Republican booth."

"Where are you at the moment?" Lou asked.

"I'm on I-94, near Ann Arbor."

"Okay, Jack and I are still in Mason, so let's share some coffee at Bestsellers. Take 94 to 127 North toward Mason, get off at one of the Mason exits, and go into the downtown area. Bestsellers is across from the courthouse, on the west side. You'll recognize it because we've met there before."

"See you shortly, Lou."

Maggie, Jack, and Lou decided over coffee and tea that Lou and Jack would show the photo of Rita Telman to Kristen Cook. Maggie would head home to Battle Creek.

Jack and Lou called first and then drove to Kristen's home who, upon seeing the photo, allowed that Rita could have been the woman at the Republican booth, but she couldn't be certain. Dejected, Lou and Jack headed for Grand Haven.

They hadn't driven a mile when Lou suggested they visit with Cindy Markle, since Lou hadn't met her and heard what she had to say. Lou asked Jack to lead the interview. Jack called Cindy at work, and they agreed to meet in the courthouse cafeteria.

After introducing Cindy to Lou, Jack said, "Nice to see you again, Cindy. Mr. Searing and I have a few more questions."

"I told you, I want to help if I can."

"We've learned that Judge Breckinridge gave you a poor work evaluation a while back. Can you tell me about that?" Jack asked.

"The judge evaluates all of the court staff once a year, and, yes, my evaluation was pretty bad. I could have stood that, except that his secretary, Elizabeth Andrews, typed up his evaluations, so she knew what he said. And I'm pretty sure she e-mailed the details to other secretaries in the courthouse. As far as I'm concerned, he turned my friends against me. They began to act as if I were repulsive. I felt like I was in prison and unable to escape. I was miserable, and it went on for a long time. It's still that way, but to a lesser extent."

"I can imagine that would be upsetting; it would be for me," Jack agreed.

"Thank you. The court became an unpleasant place to work and the people there, including the judge, made me feel ostracized."

"I'm sorry for your pain, but thanks for speaking with me."

"I hope you solve this soon," Cindy said, shaking hands with Lou and Jack.

"Thanks. We'll leave you to your work."

Lou drove to his home, where Jack picked up his car and headed to Muskegon. When Lou pulled into the driveway, Carol and Samm were waiting for him to start the evening walk. The shore was Lou's special place to spend time with Carol and to think about the things going on in his life.

The two took turns pulling Samm in her red wagon. Oh, how Samm wanted to chase a seagull or a piece of driftwood again, but she seemed to enjoy her memories.

"I'm getting old, Sweetzie," Lou remarked.

"As am I, and every other living thing that has been moving for sixty-seven years or more," Carol replied matter-of-factly.

"I can't seem to put data and people into my brain like I used to, move them around like a jig-saw puzzle. I could almost imagine an entire case, see events happening, not in a psychic way, but in a reasoning way, based on what I was learning. I can't seem to do that anymore."

"That's what Jack is for, and Maggie, and this young Heather, who's become quite a marvel."

"I know, but I should be able to do it, and I *can't*."

"We all think we're losing our minds, Lou," Carol replied, trying her best to convince him that what he was going through was normal. "'Senior moments' happen all the time. It's natural at our age."

"I often forget what I'm going to say during a break in the conversation, or I'll be talking and suddenly can't find the word I want. And then I become aware of the silence, and the other person patiently waiting for me to finish. It's unnerving."

"Normal, Lou."

"I don't think so, not with such regularity."

"Then see the doctor, explain it to him, and see what he says," Carol suggested.

"I will. But, whatever he says, it won't change anything. I'm losing it, and I don't want to lose it."

"Looks like I've one depressed husband here," Carol replied.

"Just a bit frustrated. But, there could be consolation in knowing that I'll soon forget what I'm frustrated about." Lou laughed, and Carol chuckled.

"There's the Lou Searing I know and love," Carol said, squeezing his hand.

"Look at that sunset," Lou said, looking to the west. "Artists can't come close to capturing the beauty in this moment!"

"We're very lucky, Lou. We have each other, our children and grandchildren, Samm, and Millie. We have our health and the joy of living."

"You're right. I'll use my imagination, blow all this pity into a balloon, let it fly, and pop!"

Usually, families of murder victims badger police for updates out of frustration for crimes still unsolved, but not in this case. The Breckinridges had no children, and their parents were deceased. Bonnie's brother in Alaska and her sister Joan believed everything possible was being done to solve Bonnie's murder. Win's two sisters, one in London and the other in Moscow, both worked in embassies. Neither was putting pressure on the authorities to solve their brother's murder. Lack of family pressure did not justify an extended break, but it allowed the police, Lou, and his team respite from the sense that the community or the media were hounding them for resolution.

An interesting item on the *Lansing State Journal* web site caught Jack's attention as he scanned the electronic paper. The headline read, Domestic Union Cited for Tax Evasion. The article reported allegations that not only had the union failed to report income, but the item insinuated that money had been embezzled, revealing that a reputable accounting firm would investigate further. When Jack told Lou of his find, Lou decided to contact the IRS for permission to share information about the union leader, Wilma Simmons.

Lou called the Lansing IRS office and asked to speak to the agent heading the investigation. A clipped voice answered the transfer call.

"Agent Richards."

"Hello, this is Lou Searing. I'm assisting the Ingham County Sheriff in investigating the murders of Judge and Mrs. Breckinridge."

"Yes, we're familiar with that," Agent Richards replied.

"Our investigation has uncovered many potential suspects one of whom is Wilma Simmons, head of the union you are investigating. I'm calling to see if we can share information relevant to both cases."

"Ms. Simmons may have embezzled money from the Union treasury. And, as the leader of the Union, she will be held accountable for taxes that were not paid."

"Let me give you my phone number," Lou said. "If we can assist you, please call. And might I check in with you occasionally?"

"Yes. We'll stay in touch."

Three days later, Agent Richards called Lou.

"Mr. Searing? Regarding your offer to share information about Ms. Simmons — can you come to the Union office?"

"Yes. I know where it's located."

"Good. We'll look for you in an hour. Is that possible?" Agent Richards asked.

"I'm in Grand Haven now, so it will take about two hours to get to Lansing. Can you clear me through your security?" Lou asked.

"Yes, an FBI agent will be informed of your expected arrival, and he'll bring you to the session."

As Lou drove, he decided he needn't involve members of his team at this point. He simply wanted to hear what Agent Richards had to say.

He parked on the street, entered the office building on Ottawa Street, walked directly into the elevator, and pushed the fourth-floor button. When the door opened, a man wearing an FBI nametag asked for his identification. Once Lou provided ID, he was allowed to enter the Union office. Agent Richards nodded as he walked toward Lou, hand extended.

"Good morning, Mr. Searing."

"Agent Richards," Lou replied.

"Thanks for coming. I want to show you some papers in the conference room as well as something we found on Ms. Simmons' hard drive."

Lou sat in a red leather chair at the head of the table, a short stack of files in front of him.

"I'd like you to review this material and see whether anything there is relevant to your investigation."

"I'll be glad to."

"It shouldn't take more than a half-hour. Coffee?"

"That would be appreciated. I like it hot, regular, no cream or sugar."

"It will arrive shortly. If you need me, or when you're ready to discuss the contents of those files, just have me paged." Agent Richards left the conference room.

Lou counted seven file folders, and then opened the one on top. The folder contained five letters to Judge Breckinridge from Ms. Simmons and the judge's responses to four of them. The letters contained nothing of particular interest or value. All of them sought his support of union policies or asked him to review documents pertaining to pending legislation and the impact it would have on domestics.

The second folder contained a photo of Judge Breckinridge with Ms. Simmons and Lester Grant. Clipped to it was a copy of a memo to the judge which read, "Please review the enclosed photograph. Do you wish me to keep quiet about the animosity between you and Lester? Of the two of you, I prefer to please you. I am convinced that, should you choose to run for State Representative, we can find significant funds to assist your campaign. You know, I presume, that your wife has openly expressed support for Lester's candidacy. I look forward to your response." The file contained no response to this letter.

The third file was a couple of inches thick. Lou chose not to read the details, but to skim the material. The papers concerned a court case — a retailer's suit against a company that provided maintenance work. Apparently the retailer didn't believe the contract had been fulfilled. The retailer mentioned Judge Breckinridge as another contractor who was very displeased with the company's service.

The fourth folder contained an envelope with several amateur photographs of Judge Breckinridge and MeLissa Evans in the judge's office. The photos appeared innocent enough. Lou could see the two sitting at a conference table in the judge's office. There was no suggestion of any sexual activity, and no drugs could be seen. An accompanying note read, "If you need evidence of this affair or of shared drug use, pull these photos out of your valise. There are more. Just ask." There was no signature — no indication of who had written the note.

The fifth folder held a letter from MeLissa Evans to Wilma Simmons suggesting that Ms. Simmons cease her tactics or pay a price for her indiscretion. The letter held the threat that, if Wilma Simmons didn't stop spreading rumors, MeLissa would see to it that Wilma deeply regretted her behavior. There was no response to this letter.

The sixth file contained correspondence regarding union funds. A letter from Ms. Simmons to the Union treasurer indicated that thousands of dollars were apparently missing from the accounts. The suspect in the apparent theft was Lester Grant, legal counsel to the Union. The letter detailed how Lester might siphon money from the general fund to his own accounts. Finally, there was a reference to Judge Breckinridge's being informed of this alleged theft.

Judge Breckinridge responded with the following: "It does appear that Lester has diverted funds from your Union. I assure you that, should this violation appear as an item on my docket, I will see that Mr. Grant is punished and submitted to much-deserved public ridicule."

The seventh folder was a collection of newspaper articles concerning Union efforts to protect the interests of its members. One of the newspaper articles mentioned gratitude for Judge Breckinridge's support.

Lou's coffee was now cold. He hadn't taken one sip while he was engrossed in the information within the seven files. Lou closed the last file, sighed, and asked that Agent Richards be paged.

"Did you see anything to help in your investigation?" Agent Richards asked upon arrival.

"Yes, and no," Lou replied.

"Am I to take that as encouraging or discouraging?"

"Well, I knew there was animosity between Grant and Breckinridge, but material in the file portrays it as much more intense than I thought. And, there is mention of Mrs. Breckinridge favoring Grant in the election. So I think we need to pay more attention to Mr. Grant as a suspect. Finally the judge said outright that if a case involving Grant ever came to his court, he would see to his punishment and ridicule. That's pretty strong. Obviously these two men had no love for one another."

"Anything else?" Richards asked.

"The ill will between MeLissa and Ms. Simmons is also obvious. I need to find out who took the photos of MeLissa and the judge in his chambers. Assuming the two are innocent of an affair or drug use, the shutterbug is either spreading rumors or participating in a slam effort."

"Would you like to take the photos?"

"You don't need them as evidence?" Lou asked.

"No. The photos have nothing to do with either embezzlement or failure to pay taxes. I'll have copies made, but you're welcome to take them if they'll help with your investigation."

"Thanks. Where is Ms. Simmons as we speak?" Lou asked.

"She has requested federal protection. Apparently she fears Mr. Grant and a few of the Union staffers. She'll enter the Protected Witness Program eventually, but she's out of sight while we clear this up."

"You said you found something on her hard drive. May I look at that?" Lou asked.

"Yes. Thanks for reminding me."

Agent Richards left the room and came back a minute or two later with a printout. "I wondered if this would have any meaning to you," he said, handing the page to Lou.

Lou looked at a blueprint of the Ingham County Fairgrounds, including all electric lines and breaker boxes. "Now we're getting somewhere. This is from Ms. Simmons' hard-drive?"

"Correct."

"Was this a part of an e-mail from someone?" Lou asked excitedly. "Did she send this to anyone? Was there anything in writing related to this grid?"

"I can't help you with that. It was just one among hundreds of files."

"Do you have the date this appeared on the hard-drive?" Lou asked.

"Yes, August 3."

"And Judge Breckinridge was murdered on August 8," Lou mused.

"Is it helpful?" Richards asked.

"Yes, it might be, but while I'm happy you found this, it poses a thousand new questions. Why does she have it? Who sent it to her?

Or, why did she want it? But then, that's why I get the big bucks." Lou laughed out loud at himself.

Lou sent the photos taken through the judge's curtained windows to the Michigan State Police Crime Laboratory, asking whether they could identify who took the photos, what type of camera was used, and when the photos were taken.

Lou initiated a conference phone call with the team. "I've come across new information pertaining to our murders. As you listen, try to find the needle in this haystack that will solve the murders. I think a clue here will take us in the right direction. We're long overdue."

It took Lou about six or seven minutes to explain the contents of the file folders and the diagram on Wilma Simmons' hard-drive. When he finished, he suggested, "I open this up to the three of you. Did anyone hear anything to solve this?"

After a silence, Lou asked, "Hello? Is anyone there?"

"We're thinking, Lou," Maggie replied.

"Don't all speak at once, please," Lou said, mocking the lack of reaction to his news. "Nothing from anyone? Well, I'm surprised."

"Are you hiding something from us?" Heather asked.

Lou was puzzled by her question. "No, I truly thought one of you would get an idea from these new developments."

Finally, Jack spoke up. "I'll state the obvious: Simmons could be a major suspect. The others surround her with their issues, problems, expecting her to help them somehow."

"I agree, "Maggie replied. "The fair diagram is important. I can't imagine why the head of a domestics union would have any interest in such a thing."

"I agree," Heather said. "And MeLissa Evans is probably at the heart of the case, also."

"Lester Grant stands there, too," Maggie said.

"Whoa! In less than a minute you folks went from silence to three people being at the heart of this case," Lou exclaimed.

"Looks like a conspiracy to me, Lou," Jack said.

"Explain," Lou asked.

"Simmons wants to support the court office worker who was a domestic, so she kills the judge. Grant needs to make sure that Mrs. Breckinridge doesn't run in the judge's place, so he kills Bonnie. MeLissa thinks the judge's secretary may implicate her, so she forces Elizabeth to write the note saying Evans had nothing to do with the murder and then shoots her."

It was silent again while the three considered what Jack had spelled out.

Maggie asked, "You really think Simmons would kill the judge just because a court worker, a former domestic, got a bad review?"

"Yes. Wilma knows that killing the judge also helps Grant, which is even better reason."

The team ended their discussion without making plans to meet again. Lou thanked them for their time and thoughts.

Within thirty seconds after he disconnected, Lou's cell phone rang.

"Lou, this is Sergeant Holmes at the State Police Crime Lab."

"Yes, Sergeant. Do you have something for me?"

"The photos were taken by a man, but he isn't identifiable. You can see a reflection of the person taking the photographs on the window."

"Hmmm. Okay, thanks. Can you get the photos back to me as soon as possible?"

"Yes."

"Thank you very much, Sergeant. This is most helpful."

eighteen

Heather called Lou with a hunch about the judge's death.

"What about suicide?" she asked.

"Suicide?" Lou asked surprised.

"We've looked at every possible suspect, but we haven't considered the possibility that Judge Breckinridge killed himself," Heather reasoned.

"I'm open to a new idea. Talk to me."

"He may have asked someone to shoot him."

"A perfect revenge against a lot of people. It fits with his history," Lou reasoned, thinking seriously of the possibility. "I take it this same person killed Bonnie?" Lou asked.

"Exactly," Heather answered.

"Then who killed the secretary?" Lou asked.

"Someone who knew the secretary could identify who pulled the trigger."

"Evans?" Lou asked.

"Evans, or the person who is trying to set up Evans," Heather continued.

After several seconds of serious thought, Lou responded. "You present an interesting theory, Heather, pointing out an option we haven't explored. Thank you." Lou thought another minute. "I need to reject your theory, but not because of the common sense behind it. My belief is that the judge was driven: I can't imagine him not wanting to become state representative, a position that is a possible springboard to greater power, either in-state or national power. I think others wanted him dead far more than he would have wanted to die."

"Then who did it, Mr. Scaring?" Heather asked, frustration in her voice.

"We still have holes to plug, but I think eventually the prosecutor will charge either Cindy Markle, Lester Grant or Wilma Simmons."

A month after the murder, WILX-TV did a piece on how the Republican ticket had changed since the GOP county convention. This was the first reminder to the public that the crime remained unsolved. Lou was in Haslett visiting friends. The TV was on, and since Grant was a suspect, Lou gave all his attention to the segment.

When the television reporter interviewed candidate Les Grant in his home, Lou paid attention to every word. Mrs. Grant, sitting beside her husband, tended to a cairn terrier. Presently the reporter said, "I see you've brought your dog out to enjoy our interview." As candidate Grant started to reply, the camera panned down to the dog sitting beside his wife's feet. Above Mrs. Grant's ankle was a tattoo; the camera didn't focus on the ankle, and Lou couldn't make out the design, but it was a tattoo. *Hmmm*, Lou thought to himself, *Guess we have one more suspect.*

Lou excused himself from his friends and called Kristen Cook of the Pampered Chef. "Did you see the Lester Grant interview on television a few minutes ago?"

"No, I didn't."

"Are you busy at the moment, or can I pick you up and drive you to the TV station?"

"I'm doing laundry, but this seems important, so, of course. Are you coming right over?"

"I'm not in a big hurry. Keep doing the laundry. I'm visiting friends and can pick you up in about an hour." Lou then called the television station, talked to the news director, and was granted permission to view the segment.

When they arrived at the TV studio, they talked briefly with the receptionist before the station manager appeared. "Come on back," he said, after Lou explained about the Breckinridge murder. "I've got the Grant interview cued-up."

Lou directed Kristen's attention to the studio monitor. "Okay, Kristen, when the camera pans down to the dog, look at Mrs. Grant and her leg tattoo. Is she the woman you saw standing in front of the Republican booth the night the judge was killed?"

The technician played the news segment.

"I think she could be the one."

"You're sure?"

"I think so."

"Thank you, Kristen." Lou turned to the manager, "We'd like a copy of this segment, please. And please hold on to the original tape because the prosecutor may need it in court. Mrs. Grant is a person of interest, but please keep this in confidence. I know news people like to be first to report a story, but you'll jeopardize our investigation if you broadcast our interest in the Grants."

"We won't. You have my word, Mr. Searing."

"Thank you. And you have my promise that, as soon as this information can be made public, I'll call you so you can have the scoop."

"Thank you. Good luck in solving this. If we helped, I'm pleased to have had the opportunity."

Lou took Kristen home and thanked her for her help. After she went into her house, he called Jack.

"I've a job for you, if you're willing."

"Tell me what you need, and it will be my highest priority."

"I need to find out about Janie Walker, wife of Les Grant, the Ingham County Democratic candidate running for State Representative."

"Okay. I'm on it, Lou."

When Lou had asked the TV station manager to keep the story quiet, he had assumed Kristen would honor the same request. But, he should have asked — if not told — Kristen to keep the news to herself.

Within minutes of being dropped off at her home, Kristen couldn't control her need to gossip. She usually wasn't one to gossip but when she knew of a major suspect in the Breckinridge murder, she just had to tell someone. "Boy have I got news for you," Kristen said to a neighbor. "You remember the lady I told you I saw at the Republican booth the night of the murder?"

"Yeah."

"Well, you'll never guess who she is."

"Save me playing twenty questions, already. Who *was* it?"

"Janie Walker."

"Janie Walker killed Judge Breckinridge!?" the neighbor exclaimed.

"They haven't charged her with anything yet, but she was about as close to the gun that killed the judge as anybody could get," Kristen said, spilling the beans.

It didn't take Jack long to find information on Janie Walker. The Internet provided many helpful contacts. He called Lou with what he had learned.

"She's an interesting character, Lou. And the word 'character' hardly scratches the surface. She's a part-time personal trainer. She's also a Libertarian although she is very supportive of her husband and donates countless hours to his campaign.

"According to her web site, on the night of August 8 she chaired a meeting of Women for Reform. The meeting shows a start time of 8 p.m., but no ending time."

"Good work, Jack," Lou said. "However, I can't come up with a motive for Janie's being at the murder scene."

"How about assuring her husband a victory in the election?" Jack suggested.

"That's logical, but it isn't strong enough for me," Lou reasoned. "Killing someone and risking one's freedom, assuming mental health is not an issue, takes a stronger motive than simply wanting your husband on the ballot."

"We really don't know who was standing in front of the booth when the shot was fired," Jack replied. "We believe Janie Walker was there, but she could have been at the end of the line, ten others standing with her."

"And, furthermore, Janie did not come forward with any information."

"You'd think she'd want to cooperate, explain what she saw, if she's innocent."

"Yes, but we've encountered a lot of innocent people who don't want to get involved. She probably thinks no one has placed her at the crime scene, so she needn't step forward," Lou reasoned.

"We might as well talk to her and see what she knows," Jack suggested.

"Sounds like a plan."

Lou and Jack walked up to the front door and rang the bell, and after what seemed more than sufficient time for someone to answer, the door opened. Standing before them was Janie Walker. "Well, well, Mr. Searing and Mr. Kelly. I don't suppose you're delivering Girl Scout Cookies. To what do I owe the pleasure of your company?"

"May we come in?" Lou asked.

"Certainly. Things are a bit scattered — I wasn't expecting company. You'll have to forgive the mess."

"That's fine," Lou replied as Janie led them into a den.

"How about a drink? Scotch and water?"

"No, thank you."

"Well, then, I guess we can get down to business," Janie said. "I asked why you're here."

"Yes, you did," Lou began. "We've talked to many people about the murder of Judge Breckinridge."

"And, my guess is you've not solved it or else why would you want to talk to me?" Janie asked.

"No, we haven't solved the case," Lou replied. "But we've some reason to think several people are involved."

"So, you have some reason to think *I* was involved?" Janie asked.

"Involved, possibly, but more than likely you have information that would help with the investigation."

"I see. Well, your visit is liable to be short, and you'll be disappointed, because I don't have anything for you."

"Were you at the fair the night of the murder?" Lou asked.

"No. I was chairing a meeting of women seeking change in public policy."

"You didn't go to the fair after that meeting?"

"I'm no spring chicken. The meeting was over at around 9:30. Why would I go to a fair at 9:30 — wanting to catch the Ferris wheel? No, I came home to watch the news and go to bed, if you must know."

"And, if I were to say you were seen at the fair around 9:45 that night..." Lou broke off.

"I'd tell you that Kristen Cook had best keep her nose out of other people's lives!" Janie sputtered, then calmed herself. "Selling for The Pampered Chef sounds a lot better than pushing daisies at East Lawn."

"And, what's that about?" Lou asked, keeping his cool.

"It got back to me that Kristen is spreading a rumor that I was at the fair the night of the murder — that I probably killed the judge, too."

"Is that so?"

"Yes, that is *so*, and don't give me surprised looks, because she said that you two had talked."

"I won't deny we talked with her," Lou said. "Her booth was next to the Republican booth. As part of our investigation we showed her photos of people who know the judge. She indicated that she thought you could be one of those people. Logically, we decided to talk to you, to see if you could help us, but evidently you were not at the fair."

"And, that's why I said your visit would be short, and you'd be disappointed."

"Although you weren't at the fair, can you give us a few more minutes?" Lou asked.

"All right, I guess."

"Police have not identified the weapon used to kill the judge. Have you any ideas about that?"

"How should *I* know?" Janie asked defiantly.

"Just a routine question. And, you got home from this women's meeting around what time?" Lou asked.

"I don't remember exactly, but it was around ten o'clock."

"We've learned that Mrs. Breckinridge may have played some role in her husband's death. Can you imagine what this might have been?"

"I haven't a clue. I know she had little love for Win, but that's no secret. Everyone knew that."

"Did you know Elizabeth Andrews?"

"Sure. She was the judge's secretary."

"Have you any idea why she was killed?"

"My guess is, she knew too much."

"Knew too much about what?" Lou asked.

"She probably knew who killed the judge, and somebody wanted to eliminate the possibility she'd spill the secret."

"It was a secret?"

"Of *course* it was a secret! When anybody goes about killing people, someone knows about it."

"So, if I heard you correctly, the judge's secretary, Elizabeth Andrews, knew the murderer of the judge and his wife, and that person thought Elizabeth would tell the authorities."

"That's my guess."

"Why would the secretary speak up?"

"Reward money, hero status, revenge against the murderer, to name a few."

"The breaker box at the fair blew just before the judge was murdered. How do you think that might have happened?" Lou asked. "I mean, do you think that was a coincidence, or was it part of the plan?"

"Probably part of the murder," Janie replied.

"I think so, too," Lou replied. "Karen Scott was called away from the Republican booth to take a phone call at the fair office. But when she got there, there was no one on the line. How would you explain that?"

"The murderer didn't want anyone around, so she had to get everyone else out of the area."

"I see. Was she the only one near the judge?"

"Yes."

"I'm getting it now. The murderer gets rid of any witnesses, causes the lights to go out, and POW — the judge is dead."

"Kind of odd, me telling you this when you're the ace detective."

"Well, something can be as plain as the nose on your face, but you just can't see it. I imagine a gunshot would startle people in the area."

"A gun with a silencer, Mr. Searing. Are you the *real* Lou Searing, or are you just impersonating him?"

"I'm Lou Searing, the detective. As I said, it's just that sometimes the most obvious things are too close to see. You've been very helpful."

"Anything else?"

"Yes, one more thing," Lou replied. "We can't find the murder weapon."

"Mr. Searing, the judge had a gun, kept it in his office. Now, you try to figure out what weapon could have been used."

"If you're correct, then the murderer is someone who knew the judge had a gun in his office."

"How else could it have happened?" Janie said, lifting her eyebrows and holding her palms up. "Really, your questions show a great deal of ignorance on your part, Mr. Searing."

"I apologize if that's how you see it, but you have been very helpful. You've done a good job of explaining what might have happened that night at the fair."

"Well, I'm glad I could help."

"So, all I need now is to find out who worked with the secretary to get the gun each time. That person is probably the murderer."

"But, let me throw you a curve," Janie suggested. "You've been saying, 'The murder*er*' when there could be more than one person involved."

"Oh, great thinking!" Lou exclaimed, scribbling in his notebook. "We may be about to sit down with the prosecutor and close the case."

"So, you think you know who plotted the murders?"

"Yes, I do."

"Who, if I may ask?"

"You may ask, but details concerning a suspect in a continuing investigation are confidential."

"Oh, come on! I've helped you a lot, so it seems you could let me in on your theory," Janie pleaded. "That way I can follow it in the papers and see if you're right. I might even follow the trial. It would be sort of like watching a true-crime movie or TV show."

"Stay tuned, Ms. Walker; it might be solved sooner than you think. Oh, I meant to ask, Do you enjoy wearing a tattoo?"

"And you want to know because…"

"My wife is thinking of getting one, and I'm curious how you feel about body art."

"Tell her there are consequences to everything you say and do. To be honest, my tattoo has led me into embarrassing life-changing situations. But, more power to her. If she wants it, I say, get it. You only live once."

"I'll pass that along. Thanks for talking with us."

"Let me show you to the door."

nineteen

SEPTEMBER 10TH • GRAND HAVEN, MICHIGAN

On the way home, the case came together for Lou. He pulled into a rest area near Portland on I-96, took out a notepad, and wrote the following:

> *I believe the murderer is Cindy Markle, and Janie Walker stood beside her at the Republican booth. I don't know who set the flare on fire inside the breaker box. Wilma probably arranged the series of events; that's why she had the fair blueprint. Bet I'm right. Maybe I haven't lost it after all. Note: Janie all but explained the murderer was a woman, when she noted that the murderer was a 'she.' Twice she used the pronoun 'she' referencing her hypothetical explanation of the crime.*

Lou initiated another conference call with Jack, Maggie, and Heather. The connection was made quickly, and Lou began.

"Jack and I interviewed Janie Walker last evening. I tell you this — she had the murder described to a 'T'. Anyone else might have slapped the handcuffs on and declared the case closed, but I'm pretty sure she's innocent of the actual murder."

"Whom do you suspect, then?" Heather asked.

"I think it's a conspiracy, composed of Cindy Markle, with Janie Walker and Lester Grant as accomplices. I also think Wilma orchestrated the whole thing. But I wish we could find the murder weapon. Linking that gun to a person would go a long way toward solving this. We could take theory and make it stick."

"I have an idea," Jack said.

"What's on your mind?" Lou asked.

"I'd like you to get the photos the sheriff or state police took in the judge's office, and then I'll take my own set of the same pictures."

"That's easy, but I don't understand what you're getting at, Jack."

"Just let me follow through."

"Okay," Lou replied. "The sheriff should allow you into the office. The photos are in his evidence file box."

"I'd like to go to Mason tomorrow — see if my theory has any validity."

"Fine with me," Lou said. "Do you want me to go with you?"

"Only if you want to. It could be a wild goose chase and a waste of your day."

"All right, you go. And let us know what, if anything, you find."

Maggie spoke up. "With all due respect to my friend and mentor, Mr. Searing, allow me to play the devil's advocate and suggest another way to look at this. My theory involves Zippy and family. The judge's decision took away his life. It devastated his family as it would any time a wage-earner is removed. I think the family simply saw no hope, and their legal counsel probably ranted and raved about the judge's mistake. They didn't have the money to fight it, so like the playground bully, they simply picked a fight that we call murder."

"Does the wife have a tattoo?" Lou asked.

"She's not a rejected sorority member, so she doesn't, but that doesn't mean she hasn't a friend who does."

"You think they know how to rig a breaker box?" Heather asked.

"My guess is Zippy was the mastermind. Zippy's mechanically-minded in that he operated the Egg-Beater; he would know how to blow the circuit."

"How would his family know where the judge would be that night?" Heather asked.

"They asked Mrs. Breckinridge, and she told them."

"Maybe that's what Bonnie meant when she said she was involved but didn't kill her husband," Heather remarked.

"Okay, I'm following," Jack replied. "But why did Bonnie Breckinridge die?"

"Because she knew of the crime and had to be taken out," Maggie replied.

"And the secretary?" Lou asked.

"Maybe she provided the judge's gun," Jack replied.

"What about Evans?" Lou asked.

"She was the perfect one to be framed."

"How would the Roelof family know about her?" Heather asked.

"Bonnie, who believed the affair rumor," Maggie replied.

Lou reminded them that Maggie's theory had been presented to Denny Daly who assured him that Zippy's family had had nothing to do with the murder of the judge. Lou believed him, so, while respecting Maggie's thinking, he led his team back to *his* theory.

"Do you mind if I talk to Paul Evans, MeLissa's husband, while I'm in Mason tomorrow?" Jack asked.

"Not at all," Lou replied. "You think he's involved?"

"I have a hunch he might know something. I'll let you know what I find out, if anything."

Jack arranged to meet Paul Evans at a restaurant in Haslett called Blondie's at the corner of Marsh Road and Haslett Road. Lou obviously thought the place was special asking that he be remembered to Dawn, the owner.

Dawn greeted Jack and Paul as they entered and seated them in a booth. "Lou Searing says this is a great place for breakfast or lunch," Jack said. Lou had recommended that his team go to Blondie's Barn in Haslett, sometime while in the area.

"You tell Lou we miss him since he and Carol moved to Grand Haven," Dawn replied. "They were good customers. Lou and Carol usually shared a Reuben and fries with diet cokes with a slice or two of lime in each glass."

Both Jack and Paul ordered coffee and the special: hotcakes and bacon. Sipping hot coffee, Paul began. "So, you think I might have information about the judge's murder, huh?"

"A hunch is all. I think you might at least have heard something."

"I'll give you something to take back to Mr. Searing that will make our visit worth your time and energy."

"What's that?"

"The man who took photos of MeLissa and the judge in his office was Loren Markle, Cindy's husband."

"Well, that's one puzzle piece we can certainly use. Why did he do that?" Jack asked.

"Cindy needed evidence of the two meeting after hours. She knew the only one she could ask was her husband, because anyone else would be suspicious of her motives."

"Why didn't Cindy take the photos herself?" Jack asked.

"You got me."

"How did Loren Markle get in?" Jack wondered aloud.

"Cindy let him in. She has a key, and she would have known where they were meeting."

"As I recall, there's a curtained window between the judge's office and the outer office."

"That's right. The curtains are usually only partially drawn, and he could take photos without a flash."

"Where did the judge keep his revolver?" Jack asked.

"I don't know."

"Does MeLissa know who killed the judge?" Jack asked.

"I've never asked her, but I imagine she does. You had a hunch to talk to me? Well, my hunch is that Cindy killed the judge, his wife, *and* his secretary. It's not rocket science, Mr. Kelly."

"Well, I seldom tell interviewees what we know or don't know, but Cindy is a suspect. We have several suspects, but we can't find evidence that clearly points to one person or a conspiracy."

"I know my wife is on your list, Mr. Kelly, but I can assure you, MeLissa did not commit these crimes. In fact, Cindy is trying to frame her. Those two have never gotten along. In fact, Cindy has never gotten along with anyone — hates authority. And, another person to look at would be Grant."

"The Democrat running against Judge Breckinridge?" Jack recalled.

"Correct, a man who would fare much better with the judge out of the picture."

"Do you know who his campaign manager is?" Jack asked.

"Art Baker, of Baker's All Things Electrical. Are things falling into place, Jack?" Paul asked.

"As Lou would say, 'The remaining pieces of the puzzle are in hand, and the picture is matching the box.'"

Following his talk with Paul Evans, Jack went to the judge's office, where a deputy let him in and handed him a set of photos from the evidence file.

Using a digital camera, Jack took exact replicas of the photos taken by the state police. He put the disk in his laptop, and after an hour of comparing both sets of photos, he had almost decided his theory was entirely fantasy. He was relieved that Lou had decided not to come to Mason.

Then as he gathered up the photos, he saw something. The second row of books behind the judge's desk in the new photos contained one more book than in the state police photos. He counted the books in each row twice, to be sure. He could even identify the book that was added after the police took the photos.

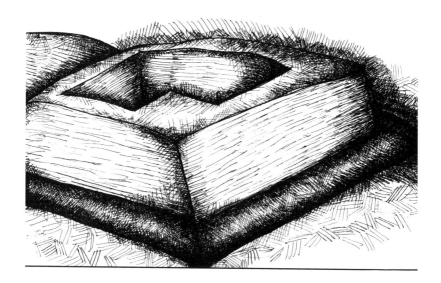

Jack stood up and walked to the bookshelf. He took the extra book from the shelf, opened it, and found a case with a revolver nestled in a cut-out the size of the gun. He didn't touch the gun, and he put the "book" back on the shelf. There was no one in the office to witness his wide grin, nor his imitation of Tiger Woods fist pumping the air after a tournament-winning putt.

When the deputy returned to retrieve the evidence photos and lock up the office, Jack showed him his photos; to document his finding the gun, Jack asked the deputy to arrange testing on the gun and the book. Possible fingerprints and a test-firing would show whether the revolver could be matched to the bullets found in the judge's body and at the Breckinridge home.

Jack called Lou with results of his interview with Paul Evans and his discovery on the book shelf.

"Art Baker, huh? Well, I'll be," Lou mused. "I always knew a campaign manager was a right-hand man, but a candidate with an electronics whiz when the opponent is killed after a breaker box blows is about ninety degrees to the right of chance."

"That's what I thought, Lou," Jack replied, and then continued, "Lou, I had a hunch that the gun had to be in the judge's office. Yesterday, I realized that a gun and alcohol are often kept in secret compartments of a desk or in a hollowed-out book. I didn't want to tell the team, thinking it a stretch. But, there was the "book" on the second shelf. I turned the gun and book over to the deputy for tests. If they find fingerprints on either the book or the gun, we'll have concrete evidence for a change."

"Excellent, Jack! Did the deputy say when test results might be available?"

"No, but he knows you need it ASAP."

"Good."

"I have one more suggestion before you wrap this up," Jack said.

"What might that be?" Lou asked.

"I'd like to study the list of items found at the murder scene. I need to settle one more hunch."

"I think I gave you a copy of the list, but I'll fax it to your home."

"Thanks," Jack replied. "And if you could stay on the line, I'll explain my hunch."

"OK, I'm sending it from my office fax to you in Muskegon."

"Lou, please look at your list and tell me about anything out of the ordinary."

There was silence while Lou reviewed the list. "One of the items was a small Bible. That seems a little out of place to me."

Jack replied. "I recall Cindy Markle gave me literature from her church when I first went to the judge's office."

"You're thinking the Bible might have belonged to Cindy, and that would place her at the murder scene."

"Yes. Lou, does the list describe any of the items? For example, was any page turned down, or is there a bookmark in the Bible?"

"There's nothing like that on this list, but the Bible should be in the sheriff's evidence file. I'll call him and see if anything has been written on it, or a page turned down, or something placed between the pages."

"Good. Let me know what you find."

Lou called the sheriff, who retrieved the Bible. "Is there a name written inside the cover?" Lou asked.

"Yes, MaLissa Evans."

"How is the name spelled, Sheriff?"

"Capital *M*, small *a*, capital *L-i-s-s-a*."

"Are any pages turned down?" Lou asked.

"Yes, a page is turned down, the page displaying the 88ᵗʰ Psalm."

"Is there anything else noticeable, you know, a prayer card, or a bookmark?"

"No, just the name and the turned-down page."

"Thank you, Sheriff. I appreciate your help."

Lou immediately called Jack to brief him.

"Hmmm, so MeLissa's name is in the front of the Bible."

"Yes, but it's misspelled," Lou replied. "You'd think the woman would know how to spell her own name."

"Cindy told me that's the way MeLissa spelled her name the day I first met her. Let me think on this, Lou. No verse was highlighted within the 88ᵗʰ Psalm, right?" Jack asked.

"That's right, but in the Bible left at the booth, the turned-down page also has the end of the 87ᵗʰ Psalm."

"Okay, let me work on this and I'll get back to you."

After thanking Jack for his call and putting the cell phone on the table, Lou carefully read each verse of the 88ᵗʰ Psalm out loud, but nothing jumped out at him. Was there any significance to the Psalm being the 88ᵗʰ? The murder had taken place on 8-8-08. If there was a connection, 88 could be the Psalm, and the 8ᵗʰ verse might be significant. Once again he read the 8ᵗʰ verse.

> *You have turned my friends against me and made me repulsive to them; in prison and unable to escape, my eyes are worn out with suffering.*

Lou typed the verse into the computer program that Heather had designed, hoping it would coincide with information obtained from a suspect. Instantly the computer brought up a quote from Cindy

Markle, *"He turned my friends against me and they began to act like I was repulsive. I felt like I was in prison and unable to escape."*

Lou called Jack back and told him of his findings. "Looks to me like Cindy Markle pulled the trigger, and Rita Telman stood next to her, sporting her tattoo. I think Rita was the woman Kristen saw at the fair. Janie Walker probably set off the flare in the breaker box."

"But, who killed Bonnie Breckinridge?" Jack asked.

"Cindy again because Bonnie knew Cindy had killed Win, and Cindy must have thought Bonnie would turn on her and tell the authorities," Lou replied.

"Okay, then who killed Elizabeth Andrews, the judge's secretary?" Jack asked.

"My guess is Cindy, once more, because I believe Elizabeth was trying to write the initials of her killer. You recall that Elizabeth sent e-mails to all the court workers containing Cindy's evaluation, infuriating her. Cindy also knew that Elizabeth had talked to me, and she may have thought we were getting too close."

"And Wilma Simmons? Is she guiltless in your theory, Lou?"

"Oh, no, Wilma was the mastermind. She wasn't at the scene, nor did she pull a trigger, but she knew first-hand of Cindy's anger. Wilma also knew Janie had something to gain from joining in the murder plot.

"And, how does Rita Telman come into this?" Jack asked.

"She never got over the judge's rejection of her when she was at Lansing Law College. She got everything she wanted out of life except membership in that elite group. Undoubtedly she had heard from Bonnie — and maybe Nicki — that the murder was in the planning stages, so she offered to help, but not directly.

Lou added, "And Nicki Nelson did not mention Rita Telman's name as one of those who had tattoos. I believe it was a cover-up as opposed to a lapse in memory," Lou stated with authority.

"Lou, I'm confused," Jack admitted. "I've heard Rita referred to both as Rita and as Artie. Is that a nickname? Or, a middle name?"

"I think it's simply her initials R — T pronounced 'Artie'."

"Makes sense to me, thanks," Jack said, once again caught by the obvious. "So, Lester played no part in your theory, Lou?"

"No, he didn't. As he said to start with, he knows how to play the campaign game. He kept his hands clean and his nose out of everyone's business."

"And MeLissa?" Jack asked.

"She was set up, *big-time*," Lou remarked. "Once you told me the name on the Bible was misspelled, I knew that someone had taken every opportunity to point the finger at her. She's an innocent victim but unfortunately, she'll always be associated with this gruesome triple murder in Mason."

"Let's get on the phone with Maggie and Heather to see if we can wrap this up."

Lou was able to connect with the women in short order. Over his speaker phone, Lou told them about Jack's interview with Paul Evans, and how he discovered the fake book containing the gun on the judge's bookshelf.

"If you're right, Lou — and I'm not suggesting you're not — that means Elizabeth's letter was not forced by MeLissa, and that Cindy undoubtedly shot Elizabeth while the two were in the office."

Heather was quick to add, "Now that we're fairly certain who was behind the killings, if we take another look at Elizabeth's letter, the jagged line could be an attempt to implicate Cindy Markle. If you look carefully, you can see a weak 'c,' leading to a wavy lower-case 'm.'"

"Good eyes, Heather!" Lou said.

Sheriff Lloyd called Lou. "I have test results for you."

"My team is with me, let me put my phone on speaker. Okay, everyone can hear. A lot is riding on your words, Sheriff. The results may fit our theory, or we may need to start on a new one."

"The fingerprints on the gun belong to Cindy Markle, and ballistics matched the revolver's barrel to markings on the two bullets."

"So, it isn't a stretch that Cindy took the gun to commit the killings, and then, needing to get rid of it, simply put it back on the shelf."

"Very logical, Lou."

"Sheriff, this is what we believe happened: court worker Cindy Markle murdered all three victims. Rita Telman was a conspirator; she was beside Cindy when she pulled the trigger to kill the judge. Janie Walker was also a conspirator, responsible for the breaker-box damage that darkened the commercial building. Wilma Simmons needed the money promised her if she planned the killings. Besides, she wanted to support a former member of the union, Cindy Markle, from a distance."

"Makes sense, Lou."

"Jack and I would like to present our theory to the district attorney. I'll write a report for you, also, detailing our supporting evidence and documentation. Every member of the team will be available to testify at the upcoming trials."

"Thanks, Lou, and thank you Jack, Maggie, and Heather. Excellent work!"

"It has been a pleasure working with you, Sheriff."

"Mr. Edman will also be pleased to hear the crime has been solved, and especially to learn that the conflict had nothing to do with the Ingham County Fair staff or the activities at the fair."

"It's time to heal, and time for us to enjoy our satisfaction in helping you and the folks at the fair," Lou concluded. "Hopefully, at next year's fair, the attention will be where it belongs: rides, cotton candy, and blue ribbons!

epilogue

Cindy Markle, Janie Walker, and Rita Telman, along with Wilma Simmons, were arrested for the deaths of Judge Winston Breckinridge, Bonnie Breckinridge, and Elizabeth Andrews. They were tried separately.

Cindy Markle was found guilty of three counts of murder in the first degree, and is now serving a life sentence without parole in a women's correctional facility near Ypsilanti, Michigan. Cindy wanted the judge dead because of his evaluation and mistreatment of her as a member of his staff. She killed Bonnie because she feared Bonnie would blackmail her. She killed Elizabeth when she happened into her office while she was absent. Cindy went to the judge's office, took the gun from the fake book, and shot Elizabeth when she returned and continued writing her note to Lou.

Janie Walker was found guilty of conspiracy to commit murder and the malicious destruction of property. She was sentenced to five years in jail with parole possible after two years.

Rita Telman was found guilty of conspiracy and sentenced to two years in prison. Rita was also found guilty of offering $25,000 to Wilma for plotting the perfect crime.

Wilma Simmons was also found guilty of conspiracy and was sentenced to two years in prison.

The idea to kill Judge Breckinridge was Cindy Markle's. Wilma said she would plan the murder for $25,000. When Cindy told Bonnie Breckinridge about her husband's infidelity and drug use, Bonnie was furious; she made it clear she would cooperate by providing information, but would play no role in carrying out the crime. Bonnie had suggested that Rita could afford to pay Wilma. And Rita had encouraged Janie Walker to help out.

At Janie Walker's trial, it was proven that she had requested a neighbor to call the fair office, ask that Karen Scott be called to the phone from the Republican booth, and then hang up. The phone call was to be made at 9:45, and Janie was to set the flare afire in the power box at 9:50 p.m. If the plan had backfired, Janie would have received a call from Cindy.

Lester Grant won election to the Michigan House of Representatives. He testified he knew nothing of the plan and had no involvement with the murders. He remains a loving husband, visiting Janie often. He has also become a strong advocate in the Michigan Legislature for prison reform.

Brenda Binder decided not to run for office in the future. Losing can be devastating, but in Brenda's case it caused her to become bitter and disenchanted with politics.

Denny Daly still lives and works in Imlay City and continues to be a model citizen.

Zippy Roelof's case was reviewed by an appellate judge, who reversed the verdict, and ordered Zippy released from prison.

Mrs. Myers and the Rives Junction 4-H Club received county, state and national awards for their work in bringing justice to Mr. Roelof.

MeLissa Evans was thankful her name had been cleared. She continues to practice law in Lansing, Michigan.

Agent Richards and the IRS determined that Lester Grant had not embezzled funds from the Union. The error had been made by the CPA firm when they conducted their annual audit.

Peter and Alice Jamison reconciled and are seeking marriage counseling. Their sons, Noah and Isaac, are doing well in school, have part-time jobs, and have taken a strong interest in playing guitar. Neither had experimented with drugs, and they were actually model teenagers who credited their mother with great parenting.

Colon Manley was diagnosed as a pathological liar. He had staged the shooting into his own home. The golf story was true, but his tales of the bass tournament and Win's unethical behavior were lies. He did fear reprisal from the judge and had taken steps to prove he had been targeted by the judge for murder.

Tommi Haynne was happy for Peter that his marriage was on the right track, but she vowed to leave Michigan in the rear-view mirror and become a permanent resident of Florida. She is now a paralegal in a firm specializing in corporate law.

Lou Searing talked to his doctor about his perception of a deteriorating mind. He was assured that occasional 'senior moments' were normal for his age and were not reason for worry.

Lou and Carol continue to walk the Lake Michigan shoreline. **Millie and Samm** seemed to sense that life has settled somewhat for

Lou and Carol; wagon rides and foot rubs can once again be expected at regular intervals.

One final note: You are probably wondering about the woman who died prior to riding the Egg-Beater. Well, her sister thought something sinister was at hand. She has hired a private detective to look into the death. The woman who died was not a drug addict, never touched alcohol, and never smoked. Eat? Yes, too much, too often, but taking drugs was totally out of character. As this book goes to print, her death remains a mystery.

The End

*To order additional copies of this book,
or any others written by Richard L. Baldwin,
please go to buttonwoodpress.com*

*This book is also available on audio.
Audio copies can be ordered by going to the
Buttonwood Press web site.*